The Christmas Wedding

An Amish
Christmas Story

J. Willis Sanders

Copyright © 2024 by J. Willis Sanders
All rights reserved.

ISBN: 978-1-954763-65-4 (paperback)
ISBN: 978-1-954763-64-7 (ebook)

Printed in the United States of America
Cover art by Getcovers.com

Novels by J. Willis Sanders

The Eliza Gray Series
The Colors of Eliza Gray
The Colors of Denver Andrews
The Colors of Tess Gray

The Clara Engelman Series
Clara's Mourning
Clara's Courtship
Clara's Choice

The Amish Holiday Series
The Forgiveness Quilt: An Amish Christmas Carol
The Easter Prayer: An Amish Easter Story
The Christmas Wedding: An Amish Christmas Story

The Outer Banks of North Carolina Series
The Diary of Carlo Cipriani
If the Sunrise Forgets Tomorrow
Love, Jake
The One Red Brick

The Hope Series
The Coincidence of Hope
The Yearning of Hope
The Gift of Hope

The Essence of Emmaline Strong

Writing as J. D. James
Reid Stone: Hard as Stone
Reid Stone: Red Rage

Writing as W.E. Needlove
Finnigan Malone's Magic Garden
Fingernail Moon

Readers, at the end of this story, please enjoy the first chapter of *The Forgiveness Quilt: An Amish Christmas Carol.*

Amazon reviews for The Forgiveness Quilt: An Amish Christmas Story

"The Forgiveness Quilt is a wonderful book that can be read in one sitting or chapter by chapter. I took it with me on a long journey, and it made the trip so much more enjoyable. The book is well written and engaging throughout, with great descriptions of the setting as well as the characters. I highly recommend this as a pre-Christmas read!"

"I just finished reading The Forgiveness Quilt by J. Willis Sanders. It was An Amish Christmas Carol. I've always enjoyed reading A Christmas Carol by Charles Dickens, so I couldn't wait to read an Amish version. I must say I loved this Amish story and it was a wonderful read!"

"This is the first book I have read by J. Willis Sanders but will not be the last. A very uplifting and inspiring book."

"This book touched my heart and my life…. This book also is an inspiration for forgiveness. It is a wonderful read. You will certainly enjoy it."

Foreword

When I first started writing novels with Amish characters, my research astonished me. If there's one thing I've learned about them, it's how they are as varied as us *Englisch* folks. For one thing, while some communities follow the same or similar *Ordnungs*, which are the rules they live by, those rules can vary. Also, the leaders in those communities—bishops, ministers, and deacons—often create new rules using feedback from the people in their communities.

For example, some communities shun electricity, while some, such as the Beachy Amish Mennonites, use any technology except television and radio. Another interesting aspect of Amish communities, one verified with research and from speaking with people who know them, is how, even though they believe in Jesus, they don't believe faith in Him is the way to Heaven. Instead, they believe the final decision is left up to God. Of course, they have the right to believe however they choose. The only reason I mention this is because I use that difference as a plot device in this book, and I want to make sure readers understand it.

Thank you for your readership. It means more to me than I can say.

J. Willis Sanders

Amish Word Definitions

Traditional Amish communities speak what's known as Pennsylvania Dutch. Authors of Amish fiction make their books more authentic by adding these words to their narratives. Many are self-explanatory, while some may not be. To clarify their meanings, here's a list of Amish words you might see in this story. There are alternative spellings for some of them, but I'm using these.

Daed — Dad
Mamm — Mom
Fraa — Wife
Schwester — Sister
Bruder — Brother
Dochder — Daughter
Sohn — Son
Denki — Thank you
Englisch — English. The Amish describe non-Amish people as *Englisch.*
Gott — God
Gute — Good
Gute daag — Good day
Gute nacht — Good night
Gute mariye — *Good morning*
Jah — Yes
Wunderbaar — Wonderful
Grossdaddi — Grandfather
Mammi — Grandmother

The Christmas Wedding

Chapter 1

Jared

On a spring afternoon, I stood on one side of a volleyball net. Ahead of me, my teammates waited for me to serve the ball. On the other side of the net, toward the back of the court, my twin brother, Isaac, cupped his hands around his mouth. "Try to get it over the net this time, Jared!"

Of course he was teasing me because the girl I'd been courting, Susan Yoder, was on his team. Standing by the net with her hands raised, she was grinning at me good naturedly.

We'd been courting for a year now. Later, if our buggy ride went well when I took her home, I planned to propose.

I tipped my wide-brimmed straw hat back and held the ball up with my left hand. "You just be ready, *Bruder*. I'll make sure it gets across this time."

Although joy filled my heart at the prospect of marrying Susan, I regretted my happiness. Mine and Isaac's *mamm* and *daed* had married later in life, and Isaac and I had spent much time caring for them because of illness. This had led to us delaying any thoughts of courting until their deaths. Now I, the first to court, would also be the first to marry.

"What are you waiting for?" Susan yelled. Red hair framed her heart-shaped face. Freckles dotted her nose and cheeks. The ties of her kapp fell across her shoulders. The sky-blue dress set her creamy complexion off perfectly. To say I loved her would be the understatement of my life. Not only did she draw me like flowers drew honey bees, we shared the same admiration for our Amish community south of Lancaster, Pennsylvania, which had only formed in the last few years because our bishop believed we should be allowed to study the Bible and the teachings of Jesus more than the former bishop thought we should.

I tossed the ball in the air and struck it with the heel of my right hand. It zoomed over the net toward Isaac, who had to dive for it. Unfortunately for him, he missed the ball and stood with grass stain on his white shirt. Unfortunately for his team, that was the final point in the game.

We gathered at the net to congratulate each other on our fine play. As everyone scattered to their buggies, Susan lingered with me. "I hope we can take a twilight ride around my folks' farm before you take me home, Jared."

Having retrieved the ball, Isaac came over, grinning because I was driving the courting buggy while he was driving the regular buggy. We'd been doing this for singings, volleyball, and other gatherings that would bring Susan and I together. We'd already eaten supper before volleyball at the home of our bishop, so a twilight buggy ride would be the perfect way to end the day, as well as to offer my proposal.

"A twilight buggy ride sounds nice," Isaac said to Susan with his familiar teasing tone. "*Bruder*," he said to me, "I'll see you at home." He winked. "Try not to keep Susan out too late."

"Just until after twilight," Susan said, worry in her voice.

"I'm joking," Isaac said. "I know Jared will have you at home at a decent time." He tipped his hat. "*Goede nacht.*"

After Isaac gave the ball to Bishop Bontrager, sitting in a rocking chair on the back porch, he went to his buggy. I helped

Susan into my buggy, climbed in beside her, released its brake and snapped the reins. "Let's go, Nick. Susan would like a twilight ride around her folks' farm." Isaac followed us on the gravel driveway. At the two-lane country road, we turned left while Isaac turned right.

As Nick's horseshoes clip-clopped on the pavement, Susan looped her arm around mine. "It's getting a little cool, Jared. You don't mind, do you? I forgot my shawl."

We were going through a bottom. The air was cooler, so I didn't mind. Unlike the behavior of the average Amish girl, Susan could be a bit forward at times. Maybe it was because we'd been courting for a while. Regardless, she hadn't tried to kiss me or anything like that. Isaac and I had heard stories of couples kissing, and we'd decided to forgo such behavior until marriage, like our folks had trained us.

Susan scooted closer. I turned to see her

expression, but she was facing forward. Instead of seeing her face, I got a whiff of fresh air in her hair.

We crossed a covered bridge, which engulfed us in its shadows, and started up the rise away from the creek. Even though the air warmed, Susan kept holding my arm, even leaning her head on my shoulder. Well, I supposed it was possible that her affectionate ways meant she loved me as much as I loved her.

A couple of miles past the covered bridge, we turned in at her folks' farm. Susan was the youngest child. Her *bruders* and *schwesters*, now married, had decided to stay in our former community. This upset her folks, but at least everyone's choices were respected enough for regular visits.

A quarter mile up the driveway, lights shown in the kitchen windows of the two-story house, painted a cheery white. Behind it and to the right was a red barn. Behind it was a chicken coop. In the twilight, I could just make out several hens either pecking at the grass or going inside for the night.

As we neared the house, Mr. Yoder came out onto the porch and waved. I stopped in case he wanted Susan to come inside. "It's a fine evening for a buggy ride," he said. "You two feel free to stay out a while longer."

"*Denke, Daed,*" Susan said. "We won't be too long."

I flipped the switch for the buggy's battery powered headlights. "Just in case a deer crosses ahead of us," I said to Mr. Yoder.

"Very smart," he replied. He covered a yawn. "We plan to turn in early. We're planting the garden in the morning." His tall frame, topped with red hair like Susan's, went inside, so I urged Nick along the driveway. It forked behind the barn and turned between a field Mr. Yoder had planted with corn and the turned soil of the garden. I loved the smell of fresh earth.

Susan, who'd slid away from me when we neared her house, slid close again. "Let's park by the pond. I love seeing the reflection of the moon in it when it rises. It's so romantic."

Susan's comment concerned me. We'd watched the moon's reflection in the pond on many a night, but she'd never described it as romantic.

I steered Nick toward the pond. On the dam, I tugged his reins to stop him. With the buggy's brakes set, I twined my fingers with Susan's. Although this was as far as I cared to show my feelings physically, she'd kissed my cheek a time or two here in the past. Yes, I'd enjoyed the lingering warmth of her lips on my face, and it made me wonder how true kisses to my mouth would feel. Each time this happened, though, I reminded myself how those questions would be best answered after our wedding.

Susan sighed. "I love it here." She kissed my cheek, lingering longer than usual. "I love it more because you're here." She raised a hand to my shirt, fingered the top hook and eye closure for a moment, and took my hat off. Then she ran her fingers through my hair. "I love your blond curls. They feel so soft between my fingers." She fingered the hook and eye closure again. "Do you have blond hair on your chest?" She giggled. "Don't think bad of me, but I sometimes imagine how you look without a shirt." She paused. "Well, I imagine other things, but I shouldn't say what."

I admit to imagining our honeymoon night, but I'd be too embarrassed to admit it to Susan. Unlike her, us plain folk are supposed to control such urges.

She palmed my cheek, turned my face toward her, and eased closer. Her breath warmed my lips. Her eyes closed. I pulled away before she kissed me. "Susan, I'm flattered by your affection, but it isn't right for unmarried Amish couples to share this kind of physical intimacy."

Her slightly open mouth puckered into a pout. "But I'm just showing you how much I love you. What's wrong with that?"

Before I could answer, she crossed her arms across her chest. "We both know other couples who do more than kiss before they're married. Why are you such a prude, Jared? It makes me wonder if you love me."

Susan calling me a prude shocked me. "I don't want to do more than hold your hand because I respect you. That means I love you. Do you understand?"

She smiled softly. "I haven't thought about love like that. Yes, you're right. Respect is important." She looped her arm around mine again and lay her head on my shoulder, content, I supposed, with my explanation.

The twilight continued to darken. In the cattails growing near the pond's dam, a bullfrog gave a resounding croak. Behind us, in last year's fallen leaves beneath oaks and maples, crickets began chirping.

At times like these, Susan often said she loved those things as much as I did, another thing that told me we shared enough qualities to make a good match.

In the distance, across the highway and over the woods lining it, the glow of the moon announced its rising. I waited until it rose fully, reflecting in the pond perfectly, before I lifted Susan's chin with my fingertips. "Susan, I love you more than I can say. Would you do me the honor of marrying me?"

Without any warning whatsoever, she wrapped her arms around my neck, kissed me soundly, and pressed her cheek to mine. "Oh, Jared. Yes, I'll marry you." She pulled away to meet my gaze. "Can we plan for the first Tuesday in November? Please say we can. If you make me wait any longer, I won't be able to stand it."

Although I told her the first Tuesday in November would be fine, her excitement made me wonder if she were more concerned with waiting to marry or with waiting to do more than hold hands.

After another kiss to my lips, she settled down to snuggle against me again. "We'll have such a blessed life. Your house is big enough for us and our children, and we can build Isaac a house close by for our privacy."

Neither Isaac nor myself had brought up the subject of living arrangements if one of us married. My *bruder* and I were close, and I'd rather he live under the same roof as we had with our folks. We needed to discuss it soon. Surprises like that often turned into family quarrels, and the last thing I wanted was to quarrel with Isaac.

Susan tugged my arm. "You're quiet. I thought you'd be as happy as me after you proposed."

"Oh, I'm happy." I patted her hand. "Maybe I'm quiet because I've looked forward to marrying you for so long that I'm in shock that it's going to finally happen."

A frown creased Susan's lips. "Can't you think of a better word than shock? I much prefer the word excited." She fingered the top hook and eye closure on my shirt again. "Like the excitement we'll feel during our honeymoon. I can hardly wait." She rubbed my leg. "If it were the end of October, we wouldn't have to wait. It would be close enough for no one to question our starting a family before November."

Talk about shock! Susan, the girl I loved and wanted to marry, was actually saying she wanted to do what married couples do before our wedding.

She rubbed my leg again. "We don't have to wait, you know. I think it's silly for the Amish to only get married in November and December. What's wrong with getting married whenever a couple wants to get married? That's how the *Englisch* do it."

Even more shock! "Susan, please tell me you're not serious. I love you and want you that way, but not until we're married."

Like earlier, she giggled. "Oh, Jared, you're so easy to tease. I wouldn't dream of doing such a tempting thing."

It was my turn to question her use of a word. In this case, "terrible" fit much better than "tempting." Regardless, if she truly were teasing me, it would ease my mind. Unfortunately, there was no way to know that.

Except for the bullfrogs croaking, the crickets chirping, and a breeze rustling in the cattails, the night grew quiet.

Shame for doubting the love of my life filled my heart. I knew we'd have a fine marriage, so what was troubling me?

Settling back onto the buggy's seat, I placed my arm around Susan's shoulders and pulled her close. No, such a simple sign of affection wasn't so bad. If I'd shown it long ago, maybe Susan wouldn't have resorted to kisses to my lips.

The moon rose higher. The bullfrogs

ended their croaking. The crickets gave a few final chirps before stopping. I kissed Susan's forehead. "I better get you home. We don't want your *daed* thinking the wrong thing."

In the driveway in front of the house, I noticed all the lights were out except for the flickering flame of a lamp on a table in the family room. I helped Susan down from the buggy. "I see your folks are asleep. When will you tell them our news?"

"Let's keep it to ourselves for a while. It's only the end of May, so we'll have plenty of time to plan the wedding before November."

"What about Isaac?" I asked. "I'd like to get his opinion on our living arrangements after the wedding."

Susan looked up at me. Moonlight reflected in her green eyes. "Maybe my brain was *ferhoodled* when I suggested he move out. I know how close you two are."

To let her know how happy she'd made

me, I beamed a smile. "*Ach,* aren't you the sweetest girl in our community. Thank you for thinking of mine and Isaac's feelings. It means a lot to me."

"Good. That means you don't have to tell him unless you want to. As close as you two are, I doubt if you could keep the news to yourself anyway." Susan raised on tiptoe to give me a quick kiss. Let that be a reminder of how wonderful our first night together as husband and wife will be. *Goede nacht.*"

As Nick clip-clopped home, a hint of doubt crept into me about marrying Susan, and I despised it. I'd dated two girls before *mamm* and *daed* left Isaac and I. A short time after our first dates, both said they weren't sure about marriage because they hadn't taken their vows, and they were considering leaving our community to live in the world of the *Englisch.* Isaac experienced the same with one girl, and we often discussed why Amish youth were looking to the outside world for happiness when happiness was so abundant otherwise. As far as despising my doubts about marrying Susan, my past with those other girls said I should be filled with gratitude for her. Not only had she taken her vows, she loved the Amish way of life, and I admired those qualities in her. She didn't mind the hard work of farm life, and she adored her cousins, especially the babies. Yes indeed, she would make a wonderful wife and mother, so I needed to toss my doubts aside.

At home, I unharnessed the buggy in the barn and let Nick into the pasture with the milk cow and our other three horses.

The two windows beneath the porch shone with orange lamplight, so Isaac was likely up late, working on business plans for the farm. Although we were twins, he had the head for numbers while I had the head for hard work. Regardless, our skills complimented each other, and we hoped to make the farm profitable again after spending so much time taking care of our ailing parents.

When I opened the door, he looked up from the oak dining table. "Ah, Mr. Romance has returned. I hope you and Susan enjoyed your twilight buggy ride."

"We did," I said, hanging my hat on one of several pegs by the door. Seeing a cup of coffee beside his paperwork, I poured one for myself and sat across from him. "It's early enough in the season to plant crops. Have you decided on what we should grow?"

Isaac's pencil stopped scribbling. "Something to regrow our bank account, you mean." He tapped the pencil eraser on the table once, a familiar sign of his seriousness. "I've been speaking with some of our fellow farmers. They say corn and soybeans sold well last fall."

I swallowed coffee. "Does that mean they'll do well this fall?"

"That's what they think. You know

those fields on the hillside behind the farm? What do you think of planting apple trees?"

The idea gave me mixed feelings. "You never mentioned planting apple trees before."

"Consider it money for our future." My *bruder* gave me a sly grin. "And for the future of yours and Susan's children."

"And your children as well, *Bruder*. That reminds me … I saw you speaking to Fanny at the volleyball game. Do you really want to marry Bishop Bontrager's daughter? He might make you a minister or a deacon, and we've got too much work to do for that."

Isaac barked a laugh. "I was just talking to Fanny, Jared. That doesn't mean I'll court her, much less marry her."

"I don't know," I teased. "Those blue eyes sure were twinkling at you."

A faraway look entered my *bruder's* eyes. "She certainly is lovely, the way her blonde hair frames her face beneath her kapp."

I reached across the table to pat his hand. "Enough of our romantic adventures. Do we have enough money to plant corn and soybeans this year? Oh, and to plant an apple orchard as well?"

"It'll be tight," Isaac said, his voice again serious. "We may need to wait on the orchard, and we don't have the money to hire any hands."

About to sip coffee, I lowered the cup. "We could ask some of our friends to help."

"They're busy plowing and planting like we should be." After sipping coffee, Isaac wordlessly returned to his paperwork.

I longed to share the news of Susan's acceptance of my proposal but didn't. Like she'd said, we had plenty of time before November.

After I donned pajamas, said my prayers, climbed into bed, and lowered the wick on the lamp until darkness engulfed the room, gratitude for my *bruder* filled me. Like with my head for work and his for numbers, he was more logical where I was more emotional. Since that was the case, my mind roamed to Susan's lovely face and warm breath as she kissed me in the buggy earlier. When I thought of such things, I also wished to marry before November, but I respected our Amish traditions enough to wait.

Drowsiness came and went. On the pillow beneath my head, I rested my head in my hands. Like with *Mamm* and *Daed's* illnesses and eventual passing, life had a way of surprising us with a variety of ups and downs, except sometimes it seemed there were more downs than ups.

Banishing this thought, I rolled to my side and closed my eyes. Tomorrow was a new day. I'd be better off to meet it with a positive attitude instead of a negative attitude.

Chapter 2

Joanna

Kneeling by my bed, I didn't know whether to pray or cry. This afternoon, my brother's doctor said he was in his last few years of life. When he passed on, I would be completely alone in the world, and the weight of this knowledge felt as if it were crushing my very soul.

Unfortunately, this wasn't the first time I'd felt this way.

Twenty-one years ago, when I was four, my parents moved to find another church.

When I was old enough for them to tell me about it, they said some members thought faith in Jesus isn't the way to enter Heaven, despite the New Testament clearly saying that. My parents believed the latter, so like I said, we started a new life in a new town with a new church. Yes, that could be viewed as extreme, but my parents took God's word seriously. For myself, all I remembered from the move was the confusion of packing up my toys and taking them to a different house.

I grew older and went to kindergarten and elementary school. Then, like a tornado piercing the sky on a summer afternoon, disaster after disaster struck. In my first year of high school, my brother, Michael, was diagnosed with ALS, also known as Lou Gehrig's Disease. Although the news devastated Mom, Dad, and myself, Michael remained upbeat. "Well," he said, "that just means I'll get to see my loved ones in Heaven sooner than later." We couldn't disagree with faith like that, so, despite our internal struggle, we did our best to adopt it as well.

Deciding on a career in medicine so I could learn more about caring for Michael as his illness progressed, I attended nursing school.

And then came disaster number two.

Before graduation, I was offered a job at a local clinic in Lancaster, Pennsylvania. Happy to live at home, I accepted and began drawing a paycheck.

Yes, both of those achievements were great, but I haven't gotten to the second disaster yet.

A few weeks ago, on the way home from Wednesday night Bible study, according to the State Patrol report, Mom and Dad swerved to miss an Amish buggy and were killed when their car struck a tree head on.

The word "devastated" doesn't begin to describe how the news affected Michael and I, let alone our lives.

The house Mom and Dad bought had a substantial mortgage. Since Michael never worked due to illness, he couldn't draw disability. Thank the good Lord, though, because need-based programs provided income and health insurance. Regardless of those facts, we'd lost Mom's income as a housekeeper and Dad's income as a carpenter, which made meeting our bills extremely difficult.

The house was larger than we needed, so we planned to sell it. Home care for Michael, which included an electric wheelchair and someone to stay with him while I worked, was rapidly draining what little savings we had. If not for Mom and Dad's life insurance, we would barely keep our heads above water. If things continued at this rate, we'd soon be sinking.

People around Lancaster were familiar with the Amish. I, for one, admired their work ethic and how they cared for the members of their communities. If someone was in need, that need was met. Everyone pulled their weight. Everyone contributed. Unlike too many non-Amish people, no one expected handouts when they were physically capable of earning their way.

Whenever I drove to work in my used Toyota Corolla, which my parents had frugally given me as a high school graduation present, the sight of an Amish man in an Amish buggy made me wonder if Michael and I would be happier in an Amish community. I don't say this because they would come to our financial rescue. I say this because they would value Michael and I more than many other people in the non-Amish world would. An example of this was when I would take Michael to the grocery. He loved to get out of the house. Sadly, many people either shook their heads at him in sympathy or refused to look at him altogether. The main reason he liked getting out were the children. If a parent let a child or children approach us, they usually asked why Michael was in a wheelchair. Without fail, he'd start the conversation by beaming a smile. Then, because of his slurred speech, I'd explain his illness, how he was making the best of it, and how he loved riding in his magic chariot.

"How's it magic?" most children would ask.

Michael would then tilt the control back and forth to make the wheelchair dart a few inches left and right. "See," I'd say. "Michael's chair is a magic chariot because it lets him dance." After grins, the child or children would say, "Wow, that's neat," or "Hey, that's cool."

Yes, Michael loved interacting with children at the grocery store.

During my lunch break, doggone it all, as I'd just learned after being summoned to the bank, disaster number three was headed our way.

"I'm so sorry," the loan manager said, "but the mortgage interest rate is rising.

Your parents didn't tell you it was an adjustable rate mortgage?"

I'd covered my eyes at the news. I uncovered them. "They never mentioned it. What will the payment be?"

"It's going to increase by over two-hundred dollars a month."

I thought I could manage that until Michael and I sold the house and found a much smaller one. When I told the manager, his lips tightened into a narrow line. "Did they tell you about the escrow for property taxes and insurance?"

"I'm afraid not," I moaned. "What about it?"

"Property values are rising," the manager said. "That means the rise in escrow will increase the payment another seventy-five dollars a month." He paused. "Um, there's one more thing. They took out a home equity loan to pay the deductibles on some of your brother's medical bills. Those payments start next month."

That conversation, along with the one with Michael's doctor about his time drawing near, left me where I was now, sitting on my bedside while trying to decide if I should pray or cry.

You know that saying, "When it rains it pours?" Michael and I were drowning, and I didn't know what to do about it.

On my nightstand, my ancient cell phone rang with my boyfriend's tone. "Hey, Jo. Are you there?"

Despite my insistence that he call me Joanna, he preferred to whack my name off like I'd recently whacked my brunette hair off into a pixie cut, tapering at the nape of my neck. Hey, I thought I'd save money on shampoo. You can't blame a girl for trying.

I picked up the phone. "I'm here, Tim."

"Oh, hey. How'd it go at the bank?"

Tim and I started dating two-weeks before my parents' accident. We met at work when he came in for a physical. One thing led to another, and he asked me out.

So far so good, right? No, not at all.

"It went as expected," I said, not feeling like talking about it.

"Great, glad to hear it. Look, um … I've sort of met someone …"

"Great, glad to hear it," I mimicked. "Have a nice life." Ending the call, I stuck my tongue out at the phone.

As anyone can tell, my love life was on par with my financial life. If both were a plane, they would be crashing and burning, and I mean spectacularly.

I knelt by my bed and pressed my palms together, but the words to God wouldn't come. This led to tears. Tears led to a wet pillow. A wet pillow led to me turning it over to the dry side before I finally went to sleep.

What a disaster of a day, at least until morning came.

"Huh, what?" I mumbled. I turned the lamp on, glared at the alarm clock that said 6:30 a.m., and answered my phone.

"Hello?"

"Hi, Joanna, this is Michelle. You sound like you just woke up."

Michelle was Michael's home care person. At twenty-five, having completed her degree, now dating two guys at once, she was entirely too perky.

"Yes," I admitted, "I just woke up."

Michelle arrived by seven to bathe and dress Michael while I got ready for work. If I were lucky, she'd make enough peach oatmeal—Michael's favorite breakfast—for me. If I were *really* lucky, she'd have my insulated cup filled with coffee for when I hurried out the door. Since it was 6:30 a.m. and her drive here took forty-five minutes, I asked what was wrong.

"Um, well, I thought the agency called you yesterday and wanted to check. Did they call? I thought they'd call."

Like with one of Michelle's boyfriends, she tended to repeat things. "No," I said, "no one at the agency called. Why would they?"

"Oh. I hate to say." Michelle's breath blew into the phone. "They should've called. Are you sure they didn't call?"

"I'm sure, Michelle. What's wrong?"

"I hate to say."

"You can say. Tell me what's wrong."

"You really should talk to them. It's a financial thing."

I covered my eyes. "Please, Michelle, what's wrong?"

"The automatic drafts for Michael's care haven't been approved for two months, so they're cancelling me."

I uncovered my eyes. "What if I paid you cash? I need to go to work. I can't risk losing my job."

"Sorry, I've got another client. Good luck with everything. Tell Michael I said—"

I ended the call. So much for Michelle as a home care professional, at least until I called about the hold on my checking account automatic drafts, which would likely have the same issue if tried another agency.

Since I was up, I called my boss at home. He understood, thank goodness, so he said to take off.

Just as I ended the call, the shrill sound of a harmonica came through the baby monitor on my dresser. Yes, that was Michael's way of letting me know he was hungry. Also, I'd need to take care of other things I don't like mentioning. Let's just say it involved a wash cloth, warm water, and soap. Hey, when a family member has a terrible disease, we do what we need to do.

After switching my nightgown for jeans, a yellow blouse, and sneakers and running a brush through my hair, I took care of Michael. Peach oatmeal and coffee followed while I explained about Michelle. His sideways grin told me he was glad. He didn't care much for Michelle's habit of keeping her eyes glued to her smart phone.

Done with breakfast and an infusion of

caffeine, I called the bank about my checking account. Yes, I got a recorded message. Yes, I had to keep saying, "Talk to representative." Yes, that took forever. Ugh, if this day kept going like this, who knew *how* it would end.

Finally, after I aged a thousand years and shriveled up into a mummy, an actual person came on the phone. Let's cut to the chase. That was the highlight of the phone call. The lowlight—is there a such thing as that?—was my checking account was overdrawn. Why hadn't I thought of that? Thanking the representative, I slapped my hand over my eyes. After a moment, Michael laughed. "You funny, Jo-yanna. It not dat bad. You could poop yo jamas like me."

Leave it to my brother to find the positive. "Yes, I could," I told him. "As you well know, you wear adult diapers, so I wouldn't poop myself."

"Yi know. It still funny." He steered his

chair into the living room, and I put the TV remote in a special holder on the arm of his chair. It took some work, but he eventually lit the screen and started watching reruns of Jeopardy that I'd recorded. You see, despite Michael's ALS, he was super intelligent. It was a rare day when he didn't answer more questions than the winner. He also liked doing things for himself if he could, hence my not working the remote for him.

"Michael," I said, getting his attention. "I need to restock the peach oatmeal. Do you want to try another flavor?"

He nodded, which surprised me. "Nanner."

"Banana?"

"Uh-huh."

I kissed his cheek. "Okay, buddy, banana it is."

The proverbial cupboard was bare, so I'd get some other things, too. Thank goodness for credit cards. I put his cell phone in a pocket of his chair so he could call me at the grocery if needed, told him I'd see him later, and closed the front door behind me.

As I approached the Corolla, I stopped in my tracks. The inspection sticker on the windshield was out of date. I went back inside, told Michael about it, said I better get it taken care of, and drove to my mechanic.

Since I didn't have an appointment, he worked me in. You got it, an hour later, and that was just the beginning of my car problems. The oil change was overdue. The passenger side headlight was out. There was a recall about the driver side airbag. He changed the headlight and made an appointment for the oil, saying it was also low, and asked if I'd like him to add a quart. I begrudgingly said to go ahead. The last thing I wanted was a major repair bill. Then he asked about the air bag, adding how important safety was, so he made an appointment for that. At the counter, as I paid his helper—a guy with dirty fingernails and a piercing in his eyebrow—the helper asked me out. After politely declining his offer of beer and pizza at his place, I left for grocery.

Michael and I lived on the outskirts of Lancaster, so my drive to work and the grocery took me through an Amish community. I admired their picture-perfect farms and their work ethic, but I didn't admire how some of their communities didn't teach everything in the Bible, especially how our faith in Jesus is required to enter Heaven. Still, the teachings of Jesus are about choice, so maybe many of them would eventually make that choice.

At the grocery, things went well enough. As I was rolling my cart along the oatmeal aisle and to the register, another cart crossed my path at the aisle's entrance, crashing into mine. When I reversed to let the person by, an Amish man peered around the corner at me. Blonde curls beneath a wide-brimmed straw hat brushed his ears. Embarrassment shaded his cheeks red. "I'm very sorry," he said. "What a *ferhoodled* thing to do."

I couldn't decide whether to grin at his handsome face or at the Amish word *ferhoodled,* which perfectly described our meeting. I turned the milk jug in my cart up. Before I knew it, I was offering him my hand. *"Gute mariye,"* I said, not trying to add any Dutch accent.

His blue eyes blinked. "How do you know our words for good morning?"

I took his limp hand from the handle of his cart and shook it. "Hey, if you live in the area, you're bound to pick up an Amish word or two."

"That's true, I suppose." He offered a shy smile. "I see you like banana oatmeal. I like peach, but my brother, Isaac, likes strawberry."

I enjoyed his medium-toned voice. No doubt it would make a fine baritone during the sings the Amish held. "What's your name?" I asked. "I'm Joanna."

He removed his hat. "I'm Jared. My brother and I live nearby."

"Nice to meet you," I said. "My brother, Michael, and I, leave outside of Lancaster. Do you farm like most Amish do?"

Jared returned the hat to his head. "We've been farming some, but we want to expand. Our folks ..."

I wondered why he'd trailed off, especially since his voice had taken a sad tone. Not wanting to pry, I smiled in hopes of cheering him up. "It's a nice spring day. Do you ever take people on buggy rides?"

"Some Amish do, some don't. I don't know what they charge."

His crinkling blue eyes attracted me. I started to touch his sleeve but pulled my hand away. "Could a first-time customer take a ride for free?"

For a second, his chin lowered as if he were wondering something. "Your— Well, maybe I shouldn't ask."

"Go ahead," I said.

"You have very short hair. Doesn't your neck get cold?"

I touched the nape of my neck, where my hair tapered. "It would get cold if it were winter. It's spring, so you'll have to take me on a warm day."

His lips parted. "Take you where?"

I held in a giggle. To be honest, no guy, Amish or otherwise, had affected me this way, and I had the feeling that no woman, Amish or otherwise, had affected him like me. "Take me on a buggy ride, remember?"

"Umm, well, I'm—"

In my pocketbook hanging from my shoulder, Michael's tone on my phone drew my attention. Hoping nothing was wrong, I answered it. "Are you ok, Michael?"

"I ok. Don foget OJ." He could say OJ easier than orange juice.

"I won't forget."

"Ok. Bye."

As I returned the phone to my pocketbook, Jared watched me intently.

Although the chance of us dating, or, as the Amish say, courting, was zero, I felt the need to clarify who Michael was. "That's my brother. Our parents died recently. We still live at home."

"I'm sorry to hear that," Jared said. "My folks passed away a few months ago."

"I'm sorry." I wondered if they'd been sick. Not wanting to stick my nose in his business, I didn't ask how they'd died.

"Thank you. Isaac and I miss them very much."

Question after question went through my mind. Did Jared have brothers and sisters? Was he courting anyone? Was Isaac courting anyone? Then my endless list of financial problems made me realize I should be thinking about them instead. If not, Michael and I could find ourselves without a home. Using a pen from my purse, I wrote my address on my grocery list, tore it off and offered it to Jared. "Here you go. If you ever feel like stopping by to give me a buggy ride, please do."

Giving me a tentative smile, he touched the brim of his straw hat and put the paper in his pants pocket. "Perhaps I will. *Gute mariye.*"

I knew I shouldn't, but as he pushed his cart away, I admired his broad shoulders. Why couldn't I meet a guy that nice who wasn't Amish?

Chapter 3

Jared

The morning after I went to bed with hopes of a more positive attitude, I cooked scrambled eggs, bacon, and biscuits. Isaac and I took turns between doing the early chores and cooking, so he, having already gathered eggs, was milking the cow. At the wood cookstove, I set the percolator on for coffee. During our last church meeting, when Bishop Bontrager had asked if anyone minded the use of propane stoves, no one protested. Our stove had been installed years ago, when our *daddi* had built this house. Then later, when our folks married, he and our *daed* built the *dawdi haus* next door. *Mamm* and *Daed* had offered to move there when they grew older, but Isaac and I loved having them nearby. This worked out, sadly, because we could better care for them when their illnesses worsened.

I plated the sizzling bacon, left the eggs in the pan to keep warm, and covered the plate of browned biscuits with a towel. I liked cooking because it made me feel creative. Isaac, with his teasing self, often said I'd make some girl a fine wife one day. With his mind for numbers, I often said he'd make a computer, like those at the library in town, a fine spouse as well.

Water filled the glass bubble on top of the percolator. I sniffed the steam coming from the spout. Isaac and I might have our favorite and not so favorite things, but we loved coffee.

Through the screened door, my *bruder's* cheery whistling said he was through milking. His boots clomped on the porch. In he came, carrying the pail of milk. "*Gute mariye*, Miss Lapp. Your breakfast smells wonderful, as usual." He set the pail on the counter, beside the basin for washing dishes. At the ice box, he took out butter for the biscuits.

I plated our food, poured coffee, and took everything to the table. Forks, spoons, and knives were already there, as well as a holder filled with napkins. Isaac and I sat. We also took turns saying the blessing, and it was his turn.

"Dear *Gott*, *denke* for this beautiful spring morning. *Denke* for the rain and the flowers and our community. Also, *denke* for my *bruder*. It would be lonely in this old house without him. Please bless this meal, amen." With a grin, he opened his eyes. "I started to say it would be lonely in this house when you find a wife, but I thought better of it."

I put a biscuit on his plate. "Stuff that in

your mouth, Mr. Joker."

Using his knife, he opened the biscuit and buttered it. "Not until this butter melts, *Bruder*. I wouldn't want to choke on a dry biscuit and deny you the joy of my jokes."

Our cooking included the running argument of who made the best biscuits. Mine, as I well knew, weren't the least bit dry, while his often were.

I went to the cupboard and returned with honey. When I woke, I wondered about telling him about my proposal to Susan. Since our marriage, as she'd reminded me yesterday, would change mine and Isaac's living arrangements, I thought I should get his opinion on it.

"*Bruder*," I said, pouring honey on a buttered biscuit, "if Susan and I marry, would you mind if we stayed here?"

Crunching bacon, he held up a finger for me to wait. After washing it down with coffee, he faced me. "Of course I want you and Susan to live here."

"Are you sure? We could live in the *dawdi haus*."

"Not at all." He winked at me. "Besides, you'll need room for the children when they start coming along." He patted my shoulder. "Seriously, *Bruder*, I look forward to this old house growing lively again."

It was my turn to wink at him. "You mean like when you and the bishop's daughter marry?"

"Oh, hush," Isaac said. "Fanny and I are just friends."

Done with our eggs and bacon, we ended the meal with more coffee and buttered biscuits with honey. Isaac intended to start plowing to plant soybeans and corn. Since we had four horses and two plows, I'd join him after I washed the dishes.

Taking advantage of the quiet, I told him about my proposal to Susan.

"Congratulations," he said. "No wonder you asked me about living here if you two got married."

"Are you really happy?" I asked. "I sometimes wonder if Susan and I are a good match."

Isaac tipped his head sideways. "Why do you wonder that? When you're with her, you're always smiling and teasing each other. That's a sign of a *wunderbaar* relationship."

To properly convey my doubts about Susan, I needed to share how she'd acted last night, much too forward for an Amish couple not yet married. I couldn't do that, though, not even with my *bruder*. Some things were just too personal. "Well," I said, trying to get my thoughts together, "I suppose most fellows who've just proposed might have their doubts."

"Exactly right." Isaac stood with his empty coffee cup. "I better get out into the fields. Our farm won't plow itself." At the door, he turned. "When I made biscuits yesterday, our flour and salt was low. Run into town for some before we're out."

I said I would and carried my dishes to the sink. After fetching water from the well, I heated it on the stove and washed the sticky honey from our plates. Done with all our other dishes, I hitched Nick to a small wagon we had for quick runs into town and set off down the road.

Just inside Lancaster, I stopped at the grocery store and tied Nick's reins to a post, alongside a buggy. Inside, I pushed a cart toward the flour aisle, then decided to get more strawberry oatmeal that Isaac loved so well. As I turned into the aisle, I was thinking about Susan, and I crashed into another cart leaving the aisle.

The person, an *Englisch* woman with short, brown hair and big, brown eyes, backed her cart up. Embarrassment heated my cheeks. "I'm very sorry," I said. "What a *ferhoodled* thing to do."

The woman offered a grin, and I was glad she wasn't upset. She turned the milk jug in her cart up and offered me her hand.

"*Gute mariye*," she said, without a hint of Dutch accent.

I blinked at her, puzzled. "How do you know our words for good morning?"

She took my limp hand from the handle of my cart and shook it. "Hey, if you live in the area, you're bound to pick up an Amish word or two."

"That's true, I suppose." I offered a smile. "I see you like banana oatmeal. I like peach, but my *bruder*, Isaac, likes strawberry."

"What's your name?" she asked. "I'm Joanna."

I removed my hat. "I'm Jared. My *bruder*, and I live nearby."

"Nice to meet you," she said. "My brother, Michael, and I, live outside of Lancaster. Do you farm like most Amish do?"

I returned the hat to my head. "We've been farming some, but we want to expand. Our folks ..." The pain from losing our folks could hit at the strangest times, and it sometimes made it hard to speak of them.

Joanna smiled prettily, revealing cute dimples. "It's a nice spring day. Do you ever take people on buggy rides?"

"Some Amish do, some don't. I don't know what they charge."

Joanna started to touch my sleeve but pulled her hand away. "Could a first-time customer take a ride for free?"

I lowered my chin a bit, caught off guard by her question, until curiosity about her replaced my surprise. "Your— Well, maybe I shouldn't ask."

"Go ahead," she said.

"You have very short hair. Doesn't your neck get cold?"

She touched the nape of her neck, where her hair tapered. "It would get cold if it were winter. It's spring, so you'll have to take me on a warm day."

My lips parted. "Take you where?"

Joanna smiled again. "Take me on a

buggy ride, remember?"

"Umm, well, I'm—"

In her pocketbook hanging from her shoulder, the tone of a cell phone drew her attention. She took it out and swiped the screen. "Are you ok, Michael?" She paused, listening intently. "I won't forget." With the phone back in her pocketbook, she faced me again. "That's my brother. Our parents died recently. We still live at home."

"I'm sorry to hear that," I said. "My folks passed away a few months ago."

"I'm sorry," she said, sincerity in her voice.

"Thank you. Isaac and I miss them very much."

Question after question went through my mind. Was Joanna dating anyone? Did she have other brothers and sisters? More importantly, did she have a serious boyfriend?

Using a pen from her purse, she wrote on what was likely a grocery list, tore that part off and offered it to me. "Here you go. If you ever feel like stopping by to give me a buggy ride, please do."

Her address was on the paper. Giving her a slight smile, I touched the brim of my hat and put the paper in my pants pocket. "Perhaps I will. *Gute mariye.*"

I knew I shouldn't, but as I pushed my cart away, I remembered her sweet smile and cute dimples. Though I shouldn't also, I remembered the way her blue jeans fit. Why couldn't I meet a nice Amish girl like Joanna, unlike Susan who was only interested in a boy and a girl doing things they shouldn't before they were married?

What a *ferhoodled* question, especially after I'd just thought about how Joanna's blue jeans fit.

Done with my shopping, I paid and loaded the groceries into the wagon so I could get back to help Isaac plow. Standing beside a car in the parking lot, Joanna waved and came over. "I hope you don't mind me waiting. I want to apologize about flirting with you."

Nick snorted. I rubbed his neck, warmed by the bright sunshine. "How were you flirting?"

"By asking you to take me on a buggy ride."

"Oh, that," I said, trying to sound serious. "My buggy rides are expensive, so I don't consider anything about them to be flirting."

Joanna poked my arm. "Stop your teasing, Jared, or did you like my flirting?"

I shrugged. "You'll have to find out when I take you."

Her pursed lips quirked to one side. "That depends on how much you charge."

I had no intention of charging anyone for a buggy ride, but I didn't want Joanna to know that. "You can pay depending on how much you enjoy it. Does that work for you?"

"It does." Walking backwards to her car, Joanna beamed me a smile. "I might be here

Saturday … you know, to see if someone wants to offer me an Amish buggy ride."

I nodded. "That's quite interesting. I might be here Saturday, too. You know, if someone wants an Amish buggy ride."

Without warning, my conscience said, *Hey, Jared, did you forget about Susan? If she finds out about Joanna, she won't be very happy about it.* Since my conscience was right, I ran to Joanna's car before she could leave. There was only one solution to my problem.

Seeing me, she rolled down the window. "Do you miss me already?"

"Um, do you think your brother would like to ride with us?"

Her mouth opened a bit, but I couldn't tell what her expression meant. She opened the passenger side door. "Get in, ok? I need to tell you about my brother."

Hoping the buggy beside my wagon didn't belong to someone in my community, I got in the car. The last thing I needed was to be caught with a pretty

Englischer in a questionable situation.

Joanna turned in her seat. "Actually, I'm glad you asked about Michael. He'd love a buggy ride because he hardly gets out of the house. Have you heard of a disease called amyotrophic lateral sclerosis, or ALS? It's also known as Lou Gehrig's Disease."

I shook my head. "No, I never heard of it."

"I didn't think you would because you're Amish. It's hard to know things like that when you don't have TV and internet. Anyway, ALS affects the nerve cells in the brain and spinal cord that control voluntary muscle movement and breathing. Michael has a motorized wheelchair and can only use it because he can still move his hands a little." Joanna's voice changed from clinical to sad. "On his last doctor appointment, he was told he wouldn't live much longer." She took a tissue from her pocketbook and wiped her eyes. "Life just isn't fair. We lost our parents. Now I'll lose my brother."

"I understand," I said. "I'd feel the same way if I lost Isaac. We're twins, so I'd feel like I lost a part of myself."

Joanna dropped the tissue. She raised her hands to cover her face. "I don't know what I'll do without him," she sobbed.

I knew I shouldn't, but I put my arms around her shaking shoulders. Resting my cheek on her soft hair that smelled sweetly of shampoo, I held her tighter. "Have faith, Joanna. *Gott* knows our suffering and helps us get through it."

Sniffling, she pulled away to get a fresh tissue and wipe her eyes. "Oh, I'm a mess. I hope I didn't embarrass you, crying on a complete stranger's shoulder."

A surge of sympathy washed over me—either sympathy or something else. How could I care for Joanna after just meeting her, and an *Englisher* at that. Isaac would think I'd lost my mind. Bishop Bontrager would question my commitment to our community. My folks, if they were alive, would threaten to shun me.

Regardless of all that, Joanna was a person, and I believed *Gott's* word included all people. I pressed my palm to her cheek. "You're doing the best you can under a terrible situation. I'm sure Michael loves and appreciates you."

Joanna pressed her hand to mine. "You are so sweet, Jared. When I drove to the grocery this morning, the last thing I thought was I'd have a handsome Amish guy comforting me in my car."

I chuckled. "No one ever called me handsome."

Joanna licked her lips, and I found myself wanting to kiss her more than I'd ever wanted to kiss Susan.

Susan!

I eased my hand away from Joanna's cheek, breaking the most intimate moment I'd ever shared with anyone, and sat up straight in my seat.

Perhaps sensing how we'd broken some

rule between the Amish and *Englisch*, Joanna also sat up. "I'm sorry for crying all over you. Yes, Michael would love a buggy ride. I'll meet you here next Saturday. Is eleven a good time? If it is, I'll pack a lunch."

With my guilt about Susan ringing in my ears, I said eleven would be perfect and climbed from the car. As I stood by the wagon, Joanna and I waved goodbye as she drove away.

I untied Nick' reins. In the wagon, I clucked my tongue to get him going. "Get up there, Nick. This silly Amish man needs to get his mind off of that pretty *Englischer* so I can help Isaac with the plowing.

Chapter 4

Joanna

While putting away the groceries, I told Michael about making a new friend. He nodded contentedly while drinking a berry smoothie I'd made him for lunch. Since he was confined to a wheelchair, getting too heavy was a possible issue, so he came up with the idea of berry smoothies instead of sandwiches and such.

When I was done with the groceries, I made one for myself and sat at the table beside him. Staying trim never hurt anyone.

After his last swallow, I wiped his

mouth with a napkin. "So, what do you think of my new friend?"

"Sound nicer than Tim."

"I agree," I said, dropping the napkin in the trash and setting his empty cup in the sink. "But what do you think about him being Amish?"

Michael shrugged. Then he touched a fingertip to his chest. "Matter in here."

I knew what my sweet brother meant. Before he got sick, Mom and Dad often told us that what mattered in a person was their heart.

I finished my smoothie, washed our cups and the immersion blender I made them with, and returned to the table. "Michael, I didn't tell you the best part. "Jared's going to give us a buggy ride next Saturday."

My brother's eyes widened. "Weally?"

"Yes, really. I'll make lunch. If we find a nice spot, we can have a picnic."

"Smoovie melt, Jo-yanna."

"You're right, a smoothie will melt. We can have sandwiches and chips this one time."

Michael worked his lips in and out and sideways. He usually did this when he was thinking hard about something. I told him to go ahead and ask me what was on his mind.

"Is Ja-wed hot?"

Leave it to my brother to remember the time I told Michelle about meeting Tim, saying he was "hot," meaning he was good looking. "Well," I said, not wanting to admit it and be teased mercilessly, "he's kind of cute."

Michael chuckled. "Uh-oh. Sound like twouble." His amused expression changed. "Wha you fine out bout nurse so you can work?"

I slapped my forehead. "I forgot to go by the home care place." I checked the calendar on the fridge. "I have two weeks of vacation. I'll take one and stay here with you and see what I can do about a nurse. Maybe I can get back to work after our buggy ride."

Done with our conversation, Mike steered his wheelchair to the living room, took the remote from the pocket, and turned the TV on to watch whatever game show he could find.

I mentioned his disability income earlier. Not knocking all home care nurses, but we'd tried a few paid by his disability income, and they hadn't worked out, which is why I'd been paying for Michelle at a private company. Since he and I agreed about using someone from a private company, I'd have to look for more online. Unfortunately, we couldn't afford internet, so I'd have to visit the Lancaster Public Library. When I did, I might as well start looking for a realtor so we could downsize our house to something we could afford.

I took those trips that afternoon, darn it. All the local home care companies I found had no openings. Great. Perfect. What next, like with the realtor? Yes, I wasn't being positive like a Christian. Yes, I'd try to do better, but when life beats you down, it can be hard to keep getting back up again.

After a prayer for strength, plus another for Michael's final years to be filled with peace, I visited a few realtors. Oh, they were interested all right. If I were them, I'd be interested too for a nice commission. I understood, though. They needed to earn a living like I earned mine.

At home again, I found Michael napping in his chair, his head against the custom-made rest that kept it upright. A line of drool had leaked from one corner of his mouth. I wiped it away with a tissue and kissed his hair. We were only a year apart in age, so we grew up together. For that reason, as well as him being my best friend in the whole world, I'd be devastated to lose him.

Yes, anyone reading my comment about being a Christian would ask why I didn't have friends in church, or why I couldn't ask someone from church to help with Michael. To be honest, after Michael was wheelchair bound, my parents had been the main church goers of the family. We'd taken him a few times, but it was too much of a struggle with his wheelchair. Then we started trading places on Sundays, with Mom staying with him, then Dad, then me. That worked until I decided to stay home all the time. Being the parents of a child with ALS took its toll on our parents, and they needed time at church to feel hopeful about a future with a cure.

As far as my future, including my feelings about losing Michael one day, I needed the buggy ride with Jared. Getting out in the country, breathing the fresh air and hearing the clip-clop of horse's hooves along the highway, would do me good.

So, the next day, Tuesday, two realtors came over to inspect the house. Of course they didn't warn me, and the house was a mess. Also, it smelled because Michael's adult diaper from that morning was in the kitchen trash. Talk about female wrinkled noses. Anyway, thankfully, they said not to worry about upgrading anything because most buyers preferred to do that themselves. I signed with the realtor with the lowest commission, and she left a For Sale sign in the front yard. With any luck, it'd sell soon, and my brother and I could add some cash to our depleted bank account. He brought up a good point, which was how we couldn't afford to downsize until this house sold. Then I brought up a good answer—we could rent an apartment in Lancaster if that's how things worked out.

Wednesday was laundry day. Thursday was doctor day for Michael. Friday was oil change day for my Corolla. In the kitchen, trying to decide what kind of sandwiches to make for the picnic with Jared, I called to cancel the oil change appointment. My mechanic said I better get it done soon. I said I would. Hey, pleasure is sometimes more important than responsibility, especially when that pleasure will be an Amish buggy ride with a cute guy, along with your brother who won't be around much longer to enjoy things like that.

Saturday morning, I went to the grocery. Instead of increasing my credit card balance, I used some of Mom and Dad's life insurance money to buy sliced turkey, a fresh loaf of whole-wheat bread, and a variety pack of chips because I didn't know what Jared would like. For dessert, a combination pack of chocolate chip and peanut butter cookies from the bakery should work. Michael and I liked both, so maybe Jared would like at least one of those flavors.

At home again, I helped Michael into the Corolla and backed out of the driveway. He wore a pair of jeans, a red T-shirt, and his favorite ballcap that he used to wear when he and Dad went fishing. My brother hated the next thing he had to wear when we went out, a bib to catch his drool. He didn't like it because it made him look silly. Still, he understood the need, so he took it in stride.

At the grocery store parking lot, we waited for Jared. Fifteen minutes later I started to worry. Thirty minutes later I cranked the car. "I'm sorry, Michael. I guess our buggy ride's a bust."

Michael tipped his head forward. "Id dat him?"

I'd been hearing the changes in his speech recently, something his doctor had warned me about. "Is" was now "id." "That" was now "dat." Thank the good Lord for this sunny spring day, because I didn't know how many more springs my sweet brother would enjoy.

Jared tugged the horse's reins beside us, and I rolled down the window. "I hope nothing's wrong. I was about to leave."

"I'm sorry I was late. Isaac and I planned

to finish plowing today, and I didn't want to let him down." Jared pointed. "Can you park away from the store? It's crowded near it, and we'll need room to park beside each other."

I agreed and drove to several empty spaces at the other end of the parking lot. Jared parked on the passenger side of the Corolla and climbed from the buggy. I got out to join him beside Michael's door. "I hope you don't mind helping me get Michael into the buggy."

"I don't mind at all," Jared said. He gestured to the buggy. "It's a little cool. I could've brought our courting buggy but didn't. It doesn't have a top."

Puzzled, I asked how not having a top make it a courting buggy.

Jared's cheeks reddened. "Well, I suppose so a courting couple will behave because they're in the open."

"Ah," I said, using my teasing tone. "It sounds like you have experience with misbehaving. Are you courting someone?"

"Let's get your *bruder* into the buggy. I'm sure he's tired of waiting."

Noting how Jared had conveniently dodged my question about him courting someone, I opened Michael's door. "Michael, this is Jared. Jared, this is Michael."

Michael raised his fingers in welcome. Like his speech, it seemed his motor skills were getting worse. "Hi, Ja-wed. Jo-yanna say you hot."

Jared knelt to look into Michael's eyes. "Hello, Michael. *"Jah,* I *am* a little warm in this long-sleeved shirt."

Michael shook his head. "Not dat. She say you—" Michael faced me. "You tell. Too hod."

My brother sure knew how to mess with me. "Jared, Michael's teasing me because I said you're cute. When English girls think a guy is cute or handsome, we say he's hot."

Jared winked at Michael. *"Denke* for

telling me. What do you say when a girl like your sister is cute?"

Michael snorted laughter. "She no cute. She purty."

Smiling, Jared nodded. "She is, isn't she?"

"She okay for sister. We go. I hungy."

"Good idea," I said. "I'm hungry too."

We eased Michael upright and away from the car. Jared, tall and strong, lifted him into the buggy. I took his regular wheelchair from the carrier on the back of the car and asked Jared to put it into the back of the buggy. While he did, I added our lunch bag, a small cooler with bottled water, and got in to situate Michael between us so he would lean against me. Jared snapped the horse's reins. "Get up there, Nick. Let's take our new friends on a country buggy ride."

We left the grocery parking lot. Five minutes later, we were heading out of Lancaster. About thirty minutes past the city limits sign, we took a dirt road to the left. Jared said this was the back way into his and Isaac's farm, and he had taken it to give us some privacy for our picnic. I didn't mind privacy, but I wondered if he'd told Isaac about our buggy ride, or if Jared was afraid someone would see us with him. Although those two scenarios were possible, he also might be afraid someone would see us and tell the girl he was courting, if he were courting one. It seemed possible since he'd never answered my question about him courting someone. I didn't mind. Maybe he wanted to spend time with me to see what dating an English girl was like before he committed to marrying anyone. Mom and Dad had told me to not get too serious about my boyfriends when I started dating, so my idea about Jared made sense. Then again, Amish guys usually started courting seriously in their late teens, and Jared looked to be around twenty-five, like me.

This made him even more intriguing. If I was lucky, I'd eventually get him to answer my question about courting someone, especially since that someone wouldn't like him being on a picnic with me.

Michael gradually sagged against my side. The sun was shining on his face through the buggy's windshield, and his eyes were closed. I didn't blame him. The warm sun made me feel like an old hound dog lying in the sun, too.

The road passed through an overgrown field. I caught the animal scent of Nick, as well as the aroma of his leather harness. The wagon went through a rut on occasion, causing a metallic jangle somewhere beneath us. The road curved to the right and straightened near the deep shadows of huge oaks, maples, and hickories. Two squirrels bounded from the field and crossed the road, gray tails streaming behind them. They scooted up an oak and scolded us from a limb as we passed. Beyond them, a white-tailed deer and her spotted fawn were pawing last year's leaves, probably for acorns.

I'd always loved wildlife and nature. It would be amazing if Michael and I could find a house with a view of fields and woods and the animals that lived in them. Not only would he enjoy watching the wildlife, it would take his mind off of his eventual death.

"I love it out here," Jared said. He took a deep breath. "There's nothing like the smell of fresh air."

Michael opened his eyes. "Me too, Ja-wed."

I grinned at him. "Someone was playing possum."

"No, Jo-yanna. Just re …relax…"

"I know, Michael. You were relaxing."

Up ahead, a clearing of about three acres opened into the woods. If I could build a dream house for my brother and myself, I couldn't ask for a more perfect place.

Jared steered Nick into the clearing. "I like how the woods surround this clearing, except where it opens to the larger field. I'd like to put a pond across the road. The view would make this a fine place for a house."

"An' we go fishin'," Michael said.

I've always tried my best to be positive about my brother's illness. Times like this, though, when he'd mention doing something far in the future, tempted me to tears. In his case, time was not on his side.

"Whoa there, Nick," Jared said, tugging the reins as we arrived at the deepest point in the little field. He set the wagon's brake and hopped down. The distance to the ground made me hesitate. With all the care Michael required, the last thing I needed was to fall and break a bone.

"Hold on," Jared said, coming around the rear of the wagon. "I'll help you down."

He took my hand, which steadied both myself and my nerves, and I hopped down. I got the wheelchair from the back and brought it to Michael's side of the buggy. "Your turn, little brother."

Like at the grocery, Jared picked Michael up. I steadied the wheelchair while he sat him in it.

"Over there by that big oak should be fine," Jared said. When we got there, he picked up a folded quilt from the base of the tree and spread it on the grass, surprising me with his planning. While he got Michael settled on the quilt, I returned to the buggy for our lunch and bottled waters. To steady Michael, I set the brakes on the wheelchair and eased his thin frame against one of the huge wheels. Jared and I sat beside him, ready to steady him if needed. Forming a semi-circle, we ate our sandwiches, crunched our chips, and drank our water.

Done with two sandwiches and a bag of corn chips, Jared thanked me for his lunch. "Not so fast," I said, taking the cookies from the bag. "We've got chocolate chip and peanut butter. Which do you like?"

"Two of each." Jared faced Michael. "Is your *schwester* always so thoughtful?"

I'd been feeding Michael, of course. About to give him water, I stopped so he could answer. Michael cut his eyes at me, humor filling them. "Her? She a nurse. She nice 'cept when she mean."

Jared laughed. "Oh? When is she mean?"

Michael's lopsided grin appeared. "I jus' teasin'. Jo-yanna nice all de time." After drinking water, he asked if I could help him lie down. Minutes later, curled on his side because he breathed better this way, he softly snored.

"He's had a busy day," Jared said.

I swallowed a bite of cookie. "Thank you for letting him come. It means a lot."

"Michael said you're a nurse?"

I figured we'd eventually talk about our personnel lives. Besides, it'd be a good way to find out if he were courting anyone. I told him Michael was right, and he nodded. "It takes a caring person for a job like that. I can tell how much you care by how you love your *bruder*. How old are you? You called him 'little brother' while ago."

"I'm twenty-five. Michael's twenty-four. We grew up together."

"I told you how my *bruder* and I are twins. We grew up together also. We're very close."

Jared paused. Either questions or comments filled his blue eyes. "I researched ALS at the library in town. Your *bruder* is a sick young man."

"*Very* sick," I said, lowering my chin. "His doctor says he doesn't have much time left."

Jared set his straw hat on the quilt. The breeze fluttered his blonde curls. He reached toward my hand, then drew it away as if it would burn him. "I wish there was something I could do."

Although the softness in his voice said he was sincere, the tenderness in his eyes convinced me he was courting someone. What girl could refuse him, especially one he'd chosen? Regardless, none of that mattered. We were from two different worlds, Amish and English, and those worlds never mixed romantically.

Despite that, I still felt the need to know more about him. I raised my head. "You said we're here for privacy. Are you afraid someone will see us together? The Amish interact with the English in Lancaster all the time. There are Amish tours, Amish bakeries, Amish restaurants, Amish buggy rides. What's wrong with an Amish picnic?"

Jared's cheeks flared red. "I … um. Well, I…" He swallowed hard enough for his Adam's apple to bob up and down. "I believe in helping others like Jesus did. When you told me about Michael, I felt strongly about giving him a buggy ride. For some reason that's *ferhoodled* my brain, I feel strongly about other things as well."

I reached over to touch his hand. "Is one

of those things me?"

Jared nodded. "I can't explain it. It feels like *Gott* brought you into my life for a reason."

None of this made any sense. I felt the same way, and I didn't know why either. Yes, I was attracted to Jared, but there was more between us than that. What made our situation even more unexplainable was how we hardly knew each other, let alone how I was English and he was Amish.

Maybe one more question would clarify things between us. "Jared, I'm not telling you this to make you think anything in particular, but I think you should know it. I don't have a boyfriend, and I'm not dating anyone. I know that doesn't mean anything because we can't see each other that way, but are you interested in me that way?"

Jared was picking at a loose thread in the quilt. "I am but I can't be. I'm courting someone."

And there it was, just like I thought. "Do

you love her?"

"We're engaged."

"But you're here with me. What does that say about your relationship with her?"

"That I'm a sinner who needs to repent."

I pinched the bridge of my nose. "If I ever get married, my husband and I have to be best friends before he proposes. Are you and the girl you're courting best friends?"

"Not really. We don't talk like you and I talk. We have some things in common, but not many. She acts like the only reason she's with me is because of my looks."

As good looking as Jared was, I could see how a girl without my ideas about marriage could feel that way. Here I was, thinking all Amish girls were sweet, innocent, and married for the right reasons, and I was wrong.

Jared was studying me as if he wanted me to solve his problems. I couldn't do that, but I could be honest with him.

"When you say your girl acts like the

only reason she's with you is because of your looks, do you mean she wants to kiss you?"

Again, Jared's face flared red. "She's mentioned more than kissing. Then she says she's teasing me. We Amish are supposed to be chaste until we're married. Some are, some aren't. I wish we all could be chaste. It honors the marriage more if we can. I sometimes wonder if the *Englisch* world is intruding into our communities. Then I realize it takes a strong person to control the physical part of love. If Susan really wants to go further than kissing, I'll have a serious talk with her."

While we talked, my mouth had gotten dry. I drank more water and capped the bottle. Michael was still snoring softly. Despite knowing Jared and I couldn't be together, I wanted something from him to remember this day—something even more special than what might be Michael's last picnic.

I stood and offered Jared my hand. "We won't ever have a day like this again. Walk with me."

"Joanna, we can't."

"We can and we should. If you were English or I were Amish, I think we'd have a chance at something special. Since we'll never change who we are, we deserve a simple walk on this beautiful day."

Jared stood and took my small hand within his large one, and we began to stroll in the shade of the trees, where the woods met the edge of our small field. Despite the obvious nervousness of our tentative glances at each other, they eventually included the hints of smiles.

Enjoying the fresh air Jared had mentioned, I asked him if spring was his favorite season.

"I like it and fall, but December is my favorite."

I playfully shook his hand. "December isn't a season."

"I like December because I like Christmas. *Daed* and Isaac loved decorating the house. I loved cooking with *Mamm*."

"An Amish man who cooks?" I teased. "What is this world coming to?"

Like earlier, a breeze fluttered Jared's blond curls. "Being a nurse," he said, "do you get much time to cook?"

"Not as much as I'd like because taking care of Michael keeps me so busy. He loves Christmas as much as I do. I try to make it special with turkey and all the trim—" The realization that this coming Christmas could be my brother's last one brought tears to my eyes.

Jared offered me a handkerchief. He waited while I wiped my cheeks. "I'm sorry," I said, folding the handkerchief.

"Don't be sorry for loving your *bruder*, Joanna. That proves you're a fine person with a caring heart."

I gave him the handkerchief. "The day we met at the grocery, I wondered why I couldn't meet a guy as nice as you who isn't Amish."

Jared moved a suspender aside to return the handkerchief to his shirt pocket. "Imagine that. I wondered the same thing about you."

We'd stopped when I'd started to cry. I looked away and back, afraid to say the words that trembled on my lips. When my first boyfriend broke my heart, Mom said to not worry, that the right man would come along when I least expected it. Could Jared, despite our different ways of life, be that man?

Even though our situation was impossible, I took Jared's hand again and released the words trembling on my lips. "Is it wrong of me to want to see you again?"

His lips parted. His nostrils flared. "You said today would be our last day together."

I pressed his palm to my chest, where he could feel my thudding heart. "I don't want it to be our last day together. Do you?"

Jared eased his hand away. "I hope you aren't asking me to lie to Susan. If she found out, it would break her heart."

I asked the obvious. "But would it break *your* heart, Jared? That's the question you need to ask yourself."

"How I feel doesn't matter. I'm Amish. I have to do the right thing. I can't betray her like that."

Anger heated my cheeks. "You said you and Susan might not be a good match. If that's true, and you marry her, you're betraying her anyway. Do you want to live in a loveless marriage?"

"Amish folks sometimes marry without love. It grows in time."

Stepping close to him, I pressed my palm to his cheek. "But we have a chance to make our love grow now. Admit it. You feel it like I feel it. Something amazing is happening between us. To throw it away would be a sin."

Jared's eyes widened. "Don't tell me we

have that in common too?"

"If you mean I'm a Christian, yes, we have that in common. Please say we can see each other again. We can meet here. No one will see us. We can have a picnic every Saturday and get to know each other better than we do now."

Jared pulled my hand away from his cheek. "No, Joanna. I won't compromise my principals by sneaking around with you. Not only would it be lying to Susan, it would be lying to Isaac."

What can a woman do in a situation like this? Standing right before me, Jared had turned from warm and understanding to cold and clinical. I whirled to stomp away from him. "Michael may be sick, but at least he cares about everyone whether their Amish or not. Take us back to my car."

Chapter 5

Jared

Although I was disappointed in Joanna for asking me to sneak around with her, I was more disappointed in myself for letting her think I cared enough to do that. This terrible feeling, both for betraying her and Susan, burned in my chest as if my heart were a glowing ember in a wood cookstove. Toward the end of the following week, it finally eased off, until Susan invited me to Sunday dinner with her folks.

She'd done so in the spur of the moment, after a mid-week singing at one of our minister's homes. We hadn't planned to go together, so I hadn't expected the invitation. Perhaps I was hoping she'd forgotten my proposal, perhaps not, but I was an idiot for thinking such a thing. I'd given my word, and I vowed to keep it.

Sunday wasn't a church day. It was also Isaac's day to cook breakfast while I milked the cow and gathered eggs. As we were eating, guilt at lying to him about last Saturday gnawed at my soul. In my excitement of seeing Joanna again, I'd made the *ferhoodled* excuse of saying I was seeing Susan that day. If it came up in conversation between them, I'd be caught like a rat in a trap.

Sitting at the table across from me, Isaac rubbed his nose, a habit he had when something was on his mind. He drank coffee and set the cup down. "Are you nervous about seeing Susan today?"

I swallowed eggs. "Why should I be?"

"You asked her to marry you several

days ago, yet you haven't mentioned her except for telling me about her folks inviting you over today. Don't tell me you've met another girl and you're having second thoughts?"

My fork clattered to the table. "Why would you say a thing like that?"

"I just told you why, because you haven't mentioned her. Before you proposed, it was Susan this, Susan that. If you haven't met another girl, why the big change?"

I picked up my fork. "Enough about Susan and me. I saw you sitting across from Fanny at the sing. She sure was smiling at you."

Isaac pointed his knife at me. "Stop changing the subject. You always do that when you get touchy about something."

I pressed a slice of bacon in my plate with my thumb. It crumbled into bits. "What I'm touchy about is burnt bacon. How many times must I tell you bacon should be crisp, not crumbly. It falls to pieces on a sandwich."

Pressing his lips into a tight line, Isaac shook his head. "You and your cooking. Like I always say, you'll make someone a fine wife one day."

Thankfully, my trick of changing the subject about Susan worked. The rest of the meal passed silently. After we washed and dried the dishes, I went to the *dawdi haus* to check the traps for mice. If my *bruder* kept worrying me about Susan, I might move there, wedding or not.

Unlike our two-story home with several bedrooms, the *dawdi haus* was one story with a large combined kitchen and living room and three bedrooms. *Grossdaddi* Lapp built it like this in case Isaac or myself, or both of us, spent the night, which we did as boys quite often.

I'd recently set the traps to see if any mice were coming in. The cheese still in the traps without any being tripped said the house was safe for me if I wanted to get away from Isaac's pestering. I'd also, as a matter of habit, built a fire in the wood stove's piping to check for smoke leaks. The three bedrooms, like in our home, had small fireplaces to keep them warm. In summer, screened windows created a nice breeze through the rooms, especially at night for sleeping. From mid-July through Mid-August, it could get quite warm. Not having air conditioning like the stores in Lancaster, we were used to those hot weeks for the most part.

Satisfied with the house, I found Isaac at the kitchen table, again going over his plans for the farm. He looked up at me when the screened door hinges squeaked. "I think we have enough money to plant the apple orchard this year. We must do it, though, before it gets too warm, or the young trees will grow too slow."

I admired my *bruder's* dedication to our farm. "I apologize for our disagreement this morning, Isaac." I hung my straw hat on one of the pegs by the door and sat across from him. "To be honest, I sometimes wonder if Susan and I are a good match. You and I are different in ways, but we get along well. You have a head for numbers while I have a head for feelings."

"No," Isaac said, his tone turning serious. "What you have is a *heart* for feelings. I've noticed that in Susan, with how she watches you. I thought that meant you might be a good match. If you're having second thoughts, that means you're using your head. As *Mamm* and *Daed* taught us, that's a *wunderbaar* thing to do in life."

Isaac bringing up how Susan watched me was a surprise. Although I wondered what he'd think of her wanting more than kisses, I chose not to ask. If I brought those things up, he might think less of Susan, and I didn't want that. After all, he might consider her his *schwester* if we married.

The pencil in Isaac's hand made a

checkmark on the paper. With him so busy, I decided on a nap to be well rested for my meal with Susan and her folks. In my room, I sat on my bed to remove my shoes. Lying back with my hands crossed beneath my head on the pillow, I waited for sleep to take me away from my conflicted thoughts, both about Susan and Joanna.

Honestly, I cared about Susan. She liked children, took her vows without experiencing *Rumspringa,* and worked hard on her folks' farm. Also honestly, like Joanna had said, she and I seemed to have met for a reason, yet I couldn't understand that reason. I was, however, happy to take Michael on a buggy ride. To think he might leave the world saddened me, but it saddened me more for how his death would affect Joanna.

I took my hands from beneath my head and rolled over.

Thinking back through all the time I'd spent with Susan, I admitted to that one day with Joanna and Michael being more special. Us helping him from the buggy and to the quilt warmed my heart. Such a simple thing, yet it filled me with gratitude.

Yawning, I rolled over again.

I'd also felt gratitude for my walk with Joanna. With her hand in mine, the breeze fluttering her short hair, her smile as she enjoyed the sunshine and the trees, I was as content as I'd ever been.

Shame heated my cheeks. If she were Amish, I'd break my engagement to Susan. After all, I was beginning to believe I didn't love Susan, and a loveless marriage is more of a trial instead of a blessing.

Just as my cheeks started to cool, shame heated them again. How dare I question marriage that way? If Susan and I did marry, *Gott* would surely bless our union with love, if not immediately, then eventually.

I turned to my back. My anguish from all of these thoughts was keeping me awake. I checked my windup alarm clock, and my eyes widened at the time. I must've slept, because I only had an hour to wash and dress before I left for my meal with Susan's folks.

I drew fresh water from the well and filled the basin in my room, wishing I had time to heat it. I shaved the yellow shadow from my cheeks, chin, and throat, combed my curls as best I could, and washed my underarms. I didn't like the sour smell, so I did this whenever I came in from working, usually after lunch and before supper, so I smelled fairly good for a hardworking Amish man. With laundered pants, a white shirt, black suspenders, and church shoes, I went to the kitchen, where Isaac was chewing his pencil's eraser. He didn't even notice me when I came in. I tapped his shoulder. "Difficulty is a miracle in its first stage."

He startled. "Oh, you're leaving." He tapped his paperwork with a fingertip. "I've been thinking of ways to make more money for things we need for the farm. If you and Susan live here, we could rent the *dawdi haus*. What do you think?"

"Well, if you aim at nothing, you're bound to hit it."

"You and those Amish sayings. I agree, though. If we don't aim to make more money, we never will."

After I put my straw hat on, Isaac stopped me before I could leave. "Has Susan told her folks about your proposal yet?"

"We were going to keep it quiet for a while. I told you because I thought you should know."

"Because you wanted to ask if you and she can live here. I understand that."

I opened the door. "Say a prayer for me. You never know what might be said to an Amish man by the folks of the girl he's courting. Good night."

To keep my clean clothes clean, I'd

hitched Nick to the wagon before I washed off and changed. He waited patiently by the pasture, nibbling the thick grass on this side of the fence. I climbed in the wagon, took the reins and clucked my tongue. "Let's go, Nick. Susan's folks are likely to ask me a million questions if she's told them about my proposal."

At the end of the driveway, where Nick's hooves kicked up dust, I took a left onto Charlestown Road, further away from Lancaster.

In my community here, both to the left and right, I passed well-kept farms every half mile or so. Some fields held beef cattle. Some held plowed ground, filling my nostrils with its earthy scent. Some held the green shoots of rows and rows of corn, just starting to poke above the soil.

I waved at a family in a buggy as they passed me, the combined clip-clopping of our horse's hooves a drumbeat on the pavement.

Two miles later I steered Nick into the dirt driveway of Susan's folks' farm. Their three-story house, the boards painted a bright white, were backdropped by a grove of oaks. Behind them, a huge red barn and two grain silos stood. In a pasture to the right of the barn, six horses and a milk cow grazed on grass and clover. Maybe fifty steps behind the barn, several pigs, evidenced by a whiff of their manure, lolled around, huge and pink in the warm sun.

Near the house's huge porch I stopped Nick and tied his reins to a hitching post. The screened door squeaked open, revealing Mr. Yoder. Stopping at the steps, he rubbed his beard. "Good to see you, Jared. It's a beautiful day, is it not?"

We shared a smile and a handshake. "Yes, sir," I said. "*Gott's* hand in nature is a wonder to enjoy."

Mr. Yoder leaned against the porch railing. "Don't you think it's about time you called me Steven?"

I removed my straw hat and pressed it to my chest. "I wouldn't feel right, sir."

"You're not a boy, Jared. You're a young man of twenty-five. Come now, let's not have another word about it. That goes for Sarah as well."

"I agree," Sarah said, opening the door. She gave Steven a slight smile, as if she knew about my proposal. Given my doubts about Susan and my confusion about Joanna, I didn't care to talk about it. I'd wait until they actually mentioned it before I said anything.

I followed her inside and hung my hat on a rack by the door. "Mmm," I said, facing her. "I smell something good in the oven."

Sweat beaded on Sarah's forehead from the heat of the wood cookstove. A lock of brown hair fell from beneath her kapp into her eyes. She tucked it back. "I'm making a Washday casserole. Have you ever tried it?"

I'd heard about them but not tried one. "It's like spaghetti with mushroom soup and ground beef, isn't it?"

"With potatoes, bacon, celery, cheese, onion, and tomato juice poured in." Sarah's hazel eyes darted to Steven and back. It's Susan's favorite, but I haven't made it in a while. I thought she might like to know how since—" Sarah hesitated. If I didn't know any better, she almost said, *Since you and Susan are engaged.* Her cheeks colored. "Listen to me prattle on. Supper's almost ready. Susan's washing up."

"Can I do anything?" I asked. "I enjoy cooking."

Sarah was peeking into the oven. "Those covered bowls on the counter are rolls and green peas. You can take the foil off and put them on the table."

Steven cleared his throat. "You're a guest, Jared. You don't need to do that kind of work."

Steven was older, with more of the typical Amish attitude of women cooking and doing the housework. Although I didn't think that way, I didn't move the bowls. I was in his house, so I'd obey his rules.

"*Denke for asking,*" Sarah said, taking the bubbling casserole out. "Susan can help when she's through washing."

Steven pulled two chairs out. "Have a seat. I understand you have big plans for your future."

My mouth went dry. Was he talking about farming or my proposal to Susan? "Umm ... well ..."

"I heard that *Daed,*" Susan said, coming into the room from the hall. "We invited Jared to eat, not for questions about farming."

Steven's lips pursed. Perhaps he wasn't asking about farming. Beside me, Susan set a stack of plates on the table. "If you'll put these at our places, I'll get some knives, forks, and spoons."

Cutting the cheesy casserole, Sarah looked our way. "Steven, please pour us some of your homemade root beer."

Grunting, Steven went to a cupboard for glasses, brought them and a pitcher from the icebox to the table, and filled the glasses. "Women's work," he mumbled.

Sarah brought the steaming casserole. Susan brought the silverware. When everyone sat, Steven bowed his head. "Dear *Gott*, please bless this food we are about to receive. Also, please be with Susan and Jared as they court, and give them the wisdom to make any decisions they may have. Amen."

Dread at what kind of decisions Steven meant froze me in place. Sarah got up and came back. "I forgot a spoon for the casserole." She gave me the spoon. "Go ahead, Jared. Then we can pass it around."

I added casserole to my plate and gave Susan the container. Everyone took turns with all the food until we'd served ourselves. Forks and spoons were raised and lowered, followed by sips of root beer.

Sarah's fork paused on the way to her mouth. "Jared, do you like the casserole? Susan made it *wunderbaar*, didn't she?"

I faced Susan, sitting to my left. "It's very *gute*, Susan."

"*Denke*, Jared. I'm glad you like it."

Steven drank root beer. "Our Susan will make some young man a *wunderbaar* wife one day, will she not, Jared?"

I spooned peas. "*Jah*, she will." After chewing the peas, I wondered if they'd choke me like the conversation about Susan, which was certainly aimed at me like the shotgun I used for squirrels and deer.

The conversation faltered. To my left, Susan smiled at me. Her *daed* sat to my right, at the head of the table, with Sarah to his right, across from me. I knew something was strange, and now I knew what it was. Susan usually sat to my right, near her *daed*. She smiled at me again, this time rubbing my leg. She must've moved to my left so she could do this, and I didn't like it one bit.

Unfortunately, I couldn't move because her folks would ask why.

The warmth of Susan's hand left my leg. "*Daed,* do you mind if Jared and I take a wagon ride after we eat?"

Susan must've seen the wagon through the screened door. I didn't want to take a ride for pleasure, but I did need to talk to her about touching me at the table. If her folks saw that, they might think it was my influence.

"*Jah,* a ride is fine," Sarah said. "I'm sure you and Jared would like to talk. You can leave when you finish eating. I can wash the dishes."

"And I can draw water from the well and heat it," Steven said.

Through the screen door came the faint sound of a horse's hooves on the road. Then the sound of those same hooves thudded in the dirt driveway, coming closer. Susan turned to look out the window. "Oh, it's Jacob Graber. I wonder why he's visiting?"

I knew Jacob Graber. Rumor had it that he had broken up a relationship or two in our community. With blue eyes, dark hair, broad shoulders and a toothy grin, he drew the smiles of girls at volleyball games like a sunflower drew honeybees. He'd courted one or two girls, but they always broke up with him for a reason no one ever said.

"*Ach,* I forgot," Steven said, rising from the table. "I'd invited Jacob to supper. He must be late." He went out on the porch. "Come, come," he said, his words loud through the screen door. "Did you forget about us?"

Jacob's shoes clomped on the porch until Steven opened the door for him. Just inside, he hung his straw hat beside mine. "Mmm, mm. Your Washday casserole smells fine, Susan."

I fought a frown. He seemed very familiar with Susan's cooking for someone she'd never mentioned to me.

"*Denke,*" she said, her cheeks flushing

prettily. She patted the oak bench beside her. You can sit here if you like."

Jacob sat. Susan fetched him a plate and utensils. He filled his plate and forked a bite of casserole, followed with a spoon of peas, and washed everything down with root beer. "*Wunderbaar.* I've been looking forward to this all day." He looked around Susan at me. "How are you, Jared? Come up with any more recipes?" He grinned. "I'm only joking, but word has it that you cook like a lady."

Susan reached across the wide table and tapped his hand with her fingertips. "Stop teasing Jared. There's nothing wrong with a man cooking."

In my lap, I clenched my hands into fists. We Amish aren't supposed to feel like hitting anyone, but Jacob had a way of making me regret that rule. Besides that, I wouldn't be surprised if Susan had told him about my cooking. The question was when and where had she told him? Perhaps on a secret buggy ride after one of the singings I'd missed?

Pausing his eating, Steven chuckled. "Jacob the joker. How are your folks?"

"They're fine except for reminding me how I should find a wife. I'm only twenty, the same age as Susan. I don't care to settle down yet."

The conversation faltered again. I ate my food although I felt like throwing it in Jacob's face. I'd have to pray about my anger before bed.

When the plates were clean, Sarah went to the counter by the basin and returned with a pie covered with foil. "Who would like a slice of peanut butter pie? Susan made it."

Jacob, raised his plate. "I love Susan's peanut butter pie."

The more I heard from Jacob, the more it seemed he'd been coming to eat more than I had.

I declined the pie. Feeling like I didn't

belong here for two reasons, because of Jacob's familiarity with Susan and the likelihood of she and I not going on a wagon ride, I sipped root beer while everyone else ate and talked. When they were done, Jacob patted his stomach. "It's just like I've been telling you Susan, you'll make some lucky man a fine wife one day." He stood. "Who wants to sit on the porch swing?"

"Go ahead," Steven said. "Jared looks like he has an upset stomach."

I suppose I did look that way, frowning now and then at how Susan was ignoring me over Jacob. "*Denke* for noticing that, Steven. I do have a bad taste in my mouth from something." I eyed Susan. "I'm sure your *dochder* has an idea what it is." At the door, I took my hat from the rack. "*Denke* for supper, Sarah. I'll be going now."

I thought Susan might stop me if she cared. From the sound of her and Jacob laughing as I climbed into the wagon, I doubted if she did.

Chapter 6

Joanna

Being a Christian, I knew the last few weeks were a blessing. A neighbor didn't mind looking in on Michael while I was at work. My boss let me come home at lunch to see if Michael needed anything. By then, he usually needed a clean adult diaper, and I sure didn't expect my neighbor to do that. My realtor even had an offer on the house. Unfortunately, the amount after paying off the mortgage wouldn't leave much of a downpayment to downsize. Sure, Michael and I could buy or rent a much smaller house, but who wants to live in a matchbox?

Then there was Jared. Had I come on too strong at our picnic? I guess so. That and the fact that he was Amish hadn't helped any. It's hard enough making a relationship work when you have things in common.

Friday, on my way to work, something nagged me. Had I forgotten something? I'd fed and cleaned Michael, so that wasn't it. I'd filled the car with gas yesterday, so that wasn't it. I snapped my fingers. I needed bread and cinnamon for our weekend treat of french toast.

A mile later, since I had time, I stopped at the grocery. As I was driving away, the Toyota's engine started knocking. Then, while smoke billowed from beneath the hood, all I could do was to pull over and let my boss know what was happening. Through with the call, I raised the hood. The oil leaking from a hole in the front of the engine reminded me of what was nagging me. I'd never made an appointment to have the oil changed, and it looked like my little Corolla was headed to the junkyard.

Shaking my head, I searched for a wrecker service on my smart phone. When I started dialing, the battery died. Standing by the open passenger door with my forehead on the roof, the only thing I could do was cry. Just when things were getting better, the bottom had fallen out of my life.

To my left, a snazzy sports car parked behind me. A guy with slick-backed hair, wearing a tight shirt to show off his muscles, got out. "Hey, sexy lady. You got car problems?"

My inner radar went off. I did not like a strange guy making a remark like that. "I'm okay. A friend is coming soon."

He shut his door and came my way. "Aw, now, don't be that way. Let old Phil give you a hand. If you play your cards right, we can—"

I didn't let him finish. After taking pepper spray from my purse, I aimed it at him. "Back off. I am *not* in the mood."

In the road behind us, an Amish wagon slowed until it stopped beside my car. Will wonders never cease? Jared looked at me and looked at the guy. "I don't know what's going on here, but when a lady aims pepper spray at someone, that someone is in the wrong."

Phil showed me his palms. "Hey, just trying to help. If you get your thrill from Amish dudes, fine by me." He got in his car and left. Jared parked the wagon in front of my car and climbed down to scratch his head while studying the Corolla's engine. "Judging by the oil under your car, you need a mechanic."

I put the pepper spray away. "What I need is a wrecker. I think the engine is ruined."

"You're out early. Are you going to work?"

Had I told him I was a nurse? It'd been almost a month since our picnic, and I didn't remember. "I'm a nurse. My clinic is a few miles away, but I need to get my car towed to my mechanic."

"*Jah*, Michael said you were a nurse at our picnic. I suppose your car breaking down made you forget." At the back of the wagon, Jared got a length of heavy rope. "I'd tow you to work, but that far isn't safe. I'll tow you into the grocery parking lot. You can call a wrecker. Then I'll take you to work. Is that all right?"

Relief washed away my anger at that Phil guy. "I'd really appreciate it, Jared. Thank you."

He tied one end of the rope to the wagon, the other to the front of the car. I closed the hood, got in, and turned the key to unluck the steering wheel. Without the engine running, the car steered hard, but we managed to get it into the grocery store parking lot. During the short trip, I had an idea. Since Jared would take me to work, I could charge my phone there and call a wrecker. With my nightmare of a morning, it was about time something worked out.

After locking the doors and getting my purse, I joined Jared at the front of the car. "My Amish hero. Thank the good Lord you came along. Now, if my car is shot, what I need is a another one. I just wish I could afford it." I regretted telling him my personal business. Maybe it was because I was so upset, both for the car breaking down and that jerk Phil coming on to me."

Jared untied the rope from the car and the wagon. While coiling it, he faced me. "I've been thinking about our picnic. If you think we can be friends instead of more than that, I can take you to work until you get a car."

Maybe he hadn't heard me say I couldn't afford a car. After all, he'd been under mine. I wasn't about to repeat such embarrassing news, so I let it go. "I hate to put you out. I assume you work in the mornings, right?"

"I can start work late. Jared climbed into

the wagon. Let me get you to your clinic."

Smiling, I climbed in beside him. "I sure didn't think I'd have a chauffeur to work today."

Snapping the horse's reins, Jared cut his eyes at me. Is a chauffeur the same as a driver? I never heard that word."

"It is." I paused, hoping he didn't mind me being nosy. "Can I ask why you're in town this morning?"

"I needed some socks." Jared raised a boot. "See my big feet? I wear socks out fast."

I raised my white tennis shoe. "I go through them pretty fast myself, being on my feet all day." I pinched the bridge of my nose. "I didn't think of this. I don't have a way home. Maybe I can rent a car."

Jared eyed me. "The *Englisch* rent cars?"

"Companies do," I said.

"If you need a ride to the rental place, I can take you this afternoon."

"That's a good idea. Then you don't

have to come to town every morning for me."

When Jared dropped me off, I asked if he could wait a minute. Inside, I hurried to my boss's office to ask if I could leave an hour early to rent a car. Sitting behind her desk, she checked her watch. "You're thirty minutes late as it is, Joanna."

"I'm sorry about my car breaking down. I'm going to rent one so I don't miss more time."

"I suppose."

At the wagon again, I looked up at Jared. "Can you pick me up at three? I don't want to take a chance on the rental place being closed."

"Three is fine. See you then." After a snap of the reins, Jared steered the horse away, and I went inside to start my day.

When you're a nurse, time, as they say, flies. Between new patient interviews, taking blood pressures and checking weights and heights, and working in a quick lunch, which I didn't because I'd forgotten to make a sandwich, the hours turn into minutes. I did go outside to sit on a bench, where I enjoyed the blue sky and the shade beneath a tree.

Before I went back inside, I closed my eyes. *Dear Lord, thank you so much for your blessings. With all the stress I've been under lately, I forget to do that at times. Now I have to deal with my car problems, and I'd much rather buy one than rent one. Michael and I also need a bigger place than a matchbox to live. If you can bless us with both, we'd appreciate it. Even if you don't, I know it's for the best because of my faith in you and your Son, Jesus. Amen.*

As I opened my eyes, despite the leaves on the tree not fluttering, a cool breeze chilled me from head to toe. My faith said to take it as a sign that my prayer had been heard. That inkling of doubt Christians sometimes have said it was a coincidence. My faith said to ignore my doubt because God would see me through the troubles

Michael and I were experiencing.

Deciding to listen to my faith, I startled as my cell phone rung. I took it from my purse, glad I'd charged it. Maybe this was a sign, too. My realtor was calling.

I swiped the screen. "Hi, Lucy."

"Hi, Joanna. I've got news about your house."

"Good news, I hope."

"Some of both. The customer changed his mind, but another wants to know how soon you can be out."

Although it seemed one of my prayers had been answered, the hard work of moving in a hurry when I had no place to move to would create another problem. "Well, it depends on if you've found me a smaller house yet."

"Can't you rent?"

"I'd rather not."

"This new person is willing to pay full price. Does that increase your incentive?"

The phone slipped from my limp fingers

and clattered to the ground. I picked it back up. "Sorry about that. I'm sort of shocked, so I dropped the phone."

"You don't want to miss this opportunity. Your house isn't getting much interest."

I didn't like feeling pressured. Regardless, I needed to get Michael's opinion. I told Lucy that and ended the call. What a day, which should end with me renting a car, which would start with Jared taking me to the rental place, which led to them wanting more than I could afford for a car like mine. What a mess.

Jared had come inside to wait patiently by the front window. When I asked the clerk why the rental was so high, Jared came over. "It's none of my business, but what about using a taxi?"

Taken aback at such a simple idea, I took my phone out to check the rates of the local taxi services. "Umm, they're too expensive." I put the phone away and faced the clerk. "I'll take the cheapest car you have for a week."

Done with the paper work, and with the keys in my hand, I went out to check my new ride. Beside me, Jared and his disappointment matched mine. "That's not much of a car," he said.

I glared at the worn tires, the faded paint, and the hazy headlights. "That's why it's the cheapest." I unlocked the door and opened it. It squeaked like a coffin lid on a horror movie.

Jared crossed his arms. "Do you mind if I ask why you want the cheapest car? Aren't nurses paid well?"

I didn't want to share my troubles. Still, after Jared had been nice enough to give me a ride, I told him everything, including how I needed a house to rent as quickly as possible.

Jared uncrossed his arms. "I know of a house. I need to ask Isaac and my bishop first."

Since Jared needed to ask those people, I assumed an Amish person owned the house. Then, since he had to ask his brother, I assumed it was their house. When he confirmed my assumptions, I asked if he was sure.

"I am. We need money to help grow our farm." He grinned. "How do you feel about no electricity, no running water, and cooking on a wood stove."

"That depends on the rent, smart aleck." I hated to do without those things, but the rent should be a lot cheaper.

"I'll ask Isaac. Maybe 100 dollars a month. We wouldn't want to take advantage of anyone."

The amount surprised me. Most rentals cost several hundreds of dollars. "What about a microwave, a refrigerator, and a toaster oven? It's just Michael and me. Those things would work for us."

Jared rubbed his chin. "Some people in our community use propane generators.

What if you had one of those?"

I shot my hand out. "If everyone is okay with it, you've got a deal."

Chapter 7

Jared

After I left Joanna, I started to wonder if my brain was *ferhoodled* for offering her the *dawdi haus*. Isaac would surely think that. Susan would get jealous when she found out. As far as asking Bishop Bontrager, I had no idea what he would think since Joanna and Michael weren't Amish.

Then there was my attraction to Joanna. Not only was my brain *ferhoodled* concerning her, it seemed my heart was too. I admired her love for her *bruder*, the same as my love for Isaac. I also admired how she was handling her situation, both with her financial problems and making sure Michael was cared for.

At home, after unhitching Nick from the wagon and letting him into the pasture, I found Isaac in the kitchen, peering in the icebox. He turned as the screen door squeaked open. "Do you mind telling me where you've been? It's your turn to cook supper."

I pointed toward the icebox. "There's leftover roast."

Isacc moved milk and butter aside. "Ah, there it is. Light the stove so we can warm it."

I lit the stove. Isaac brought the bowl with the roast, which included carrots, potatoes, and onions. I put a large skillet on the stove, an idea blooming in my brain. "If we had a generator, we could heat food a lot quicker with a microwave oven."

Isaac's brow furrowed. "You know we can't use microwaves."

"The Beachy Amish Mennonites use them. Bishop Bontrager might consider it if he saw how convenient they are."

Isaac cut his eyes at me. "How do you know how convenient they are?"

I added a bit of oil to the pan. "I used one to heat a sandwich in a store in town once. I appreciated not needing to build a fire in a stove. I just put the sandwich in and pressed a button. One minute later, I had a hot sandwich."

Isaac added the roast and vegetables to the pan. "Hmm, let's ask Bishop Bontrager about it when we see him. Time not spent chopping wood is time spent doing other things."

With a wooden spoon, I stirred our supper, my mouth watering at the scent of beef and onions. "I have another idea. This is one to earn the money we need for things around the farm."

Isaac was placing glasses on the table. "I like ideas like that. What is it?"

"Since you don't mind if Susan and I live here after we're married, what if we rented the *dawdi haus*? I know someone who's interested."

Isaac poured lemonade and returned the pitcher to the icebox. "I can't imagine who it is. All the Amish in our community have homes."

I stirred our now sizzling meal again. It was time to convince my *bruder* to accept Joanna. Then it would be time to convince Bishop Bontrager. I thought they would, especially because of Michael. After all, our community had formed here to freely practice our Christian faith, and what better way to practice it than to help those in need, even if they weren't Amish.

As I plated our food, I told Isaac we could talk while we ate. I said the blessing, took a few mouthfuls, washed it down with lemonade, and finally faced him. "Our community moved here to practice our faith in Jesus, *jah*?"

About to drink lemonade, Isaac lowered the glass. "You know that's why. We were thirteen when we moved."

"Then shouldn't we practice that faith by helping anyone, even if they aren't Amish?"

Isaac's eyes narrowed. "If you mean you want to rent the *dawdi haus* to an *Englischer,* I don't know what Bishop Bontrager will think of that."

"What do you think of it? This person needs our help." I hesitated to tell Isaac how the person was a young woman, but he would know eventually. "I met her in the grocery a while back. Her brother is very ill and not expected to live much longer. They have money problems. If it makes any difference, they've lost their parents like we have." I pressed my palm to my chest. "I feel strongly about this, *Bruder.* I think *Gott* has brought them into my life for a reason."

Isaac sighed. "Just how old is this young woman?"

"She's our age."

"I don't suppose she's homely."

My cheeks heated. "I ... um ... I haven't noticed."

Isaac burst out laughing. "Is this young woman giving you second thoughts about Susan? I hope not. Since she's *Englisch*, a relationship with her is impossible."

I paused, not intending to tell Isaac about my supper with the Yoders. Now, though, I thought I should. "There's another reason I'm having second thoughts about Susan. When I had supper with the Yoders, Mr. Yoder had invited Jacob Graber. He and Mrs. Yoder, and Susan too, seemed to enjoy his company much more than mine."

Isaac swallowed a bite of roast. "Do you know what you just said?"

I searched through my words. "No, what?"

"When you said 'there's another reason I'm having second thoughts about Susan,' you admitted that this young woman *is* one of the reasons you're having second thoughts about Susan. Don't tell me you've fallen for an *Englischer*."

I licked my lips. "I know better than that. Don't you think helping her and her *bruder* is the Christian thing to do?"

Still grinning from his laugh, Isaac went on. "Your—as you call it—concern for this woman reminds me of that girl from our old community you used to like when we were little boys. How old were we back then?"

I frowned at Isaac. "I don't remember who you're talking about."

He waved my comment away. "Never mind. It was a long time ago."

I ate a few more mouthfuls. "If Bishop Bontrager allows us to rent the house to her, I told her she could have a propane generator for a refrigerator, a toaster oven, and a microwave. Since she's not Amish, I think that should be acceptable."

In theory, Isaac agreed, adding how both he and Bishop Bontrager should meet this young woman, which is what happened the following Saturday morning, after I showed Joanna the *dawdi haus*. We were sitting at this table, having coffee and sugar cookies I'd made from *Mamm's* recipe. The only thing Joanna didn't like about the house was the lack of a television. After she explained how Michael enjoyed certain shows, I understood. Still, he liked to read from a stand on his wheelchair, so she thought he would be all right without television.

"This request is out of the ordinary for our community," Bishop Bontrager said to Joanna. "You said you're not married. Does that mean you invite your boyfriend over? We would frown upon that."

"I don't have a boyfriend," Joanna said after drinking coffee. "I did have one and it didn't work out. I'd rather spend what's left of Michael's time taking care of him instead of dealing with some hardheaded boyfriend."

"Ah," the bishop said, smiling. "It seems we share the same opinion of many *Englisch* young men."

"Do we ever," Joanna said. "Then again, quite a few English girls are the same. They think fancy clothes and hairdos and cars are more important than good character. I don't think that way at all. I'll take the simple life any day of the week over fancy."

"Like you, we're plain people." Bishop Bontrager chuckled. "I don't suppose you were ever Amish, were you?"

"No, sir, but my parents did teach Michael and I to follow Jesus." Joanna paused. Her eyes lowered, then raised. "Living in the area, I know some Amish bishops don't teach their people about Jesus. What do you teach?"

Isaac paused from drinking coffee. "The good bishop, along with our ministers and deacons, follow the New Testament. We believe faith in Jesus is how we enter Heaven. Our community formed here so we could do that."

"I suppose," the bishop said, facing Isaac, "we need to teach headstrong young men to not interrupt their bishop, eh?"

I elbowed my *bruder*. "That sounds like a fine idea, doesn't it?"

Isaac apologized. "Aside from my mistake, Bishop Bontrager, is it all right if Joanna and Michael rent the *dawdi haus* and make the changes they need?"

"Can I decorate for Christmas?" Joanna asked. "It's mine and Michael's favorite time of year. I want to make this one as special as possible for him because—" Joanna blinked. "Well, as hard as it is to think about, this will probably be his last Christmas."

Bishop Bontrager patted her hand on the table. "I see nothing wrong with it, Joanna." He grinned at me. "Jared will even cut you a cedar for your tree, won't you Jared?"

Isaac laughed. "As good as he is in the kitchen, he can help decorate your tree and the *dawdi haus.* You'll just have to teach him since we do very little of that."

As if the bishop were deep in thought, he tilted his head to one side. "Joanna, you say your last name is Weaver?"

"It is."

"You said your folks are no longer with us. I remember a car accident with a buggy not long ago. Was that them?"

"Yes, sir, it was. It was night. The police report said the buggy's rear lights were out because the batteries needed changing. To keep from hitting it, my dad drove off the road. He didn't have a choice because another car was coming in the other lane. I just wish that tree hadn't been there."

"I remember that," Isaac said somberly. "I know your *daed* didn't see that tree, but he saved the lives of the family in that buggy."

"I agree," Bishop Bontrager said. "They weren't from our community, but after that accident, I told everyone here to change their batteries often."

The mood of death silenced everyone. Coffee cups were raised and lowered. Cookies were crunched and swallowed. My only problem now was what Susan would think of my new friend and neighbor. Well, that wasn't necessarily true. Another problem, though I could see it as something positive, was how she felt about Jacob Graber. As much as I questioned my proposal, I'd given my word, and nothing short of disaster would break it.

Isaac stood. "Joanna, our wagon will hold plenty of furniture. When can Jared and I help you move in?"

She blinked until tears rolled down her cheeks. "I don't know how to thank you all. My prayers have been answered."

I stood and clapped Isaac's shoulder. "You won't say that when my *bruder's* snoring rattles even *your* windows."

Laughing, Susan took a napkin from the holder and wiped her eyes. "You two remind me of Michael and I before he got sick. We joked and teased almost constantly."

"I look forward to meeting him," Bishop Bontrager said. "I'll keep him in my prayers."

"As far as moving," Joanna said, "what about next Saturday? I'm having a yard sale this Saturday, so maybe there won't be so much to move."

"I think we can work it in," I said.

At that, Joanna and the bishop stood. Outside, they said goodbye, and the bishop left in his buggy. "We'll see you Next Saturday," Isaac said. "I've got to take Nick to the blacksmith for new shoes."

As my *bruder* left for the pasture, I faced Joanna. "I realize we haven't talked much about our picnic."

Her mouth twitched, probably because she knew I meant we hadn't talked about why the picnic broke up. "I apologize for how I acted, Jared. It was wrong to ask you to sneak around with me, especially when you're engaged. I … it won't happen again."

I hated the sadness in her voice. I wanted to say I was wrong, that I wanted to see if our relationship could grow into something as special as she made me feel every time I saw her. What an idiot I'd been to propose to Susan when I'd had my doubts. One thing I needed to know for sure, since she seemed interested in Jacob Graber, was if she really wanted to marry me or not. No, that made no since, with the way her folks were hinting about it during that supper.

Joanna touched my sleeve. "Are you all right? You look like you're thinking hard about something."

"I'm fine. Thank you for clearing things up between us. Now we can be friends, *jah?*"

She flashed me a beautiful smile. "Only if you know where I can buy a propane generator. I thought they all ran on gas."

I told her the home improvement stores

in the area sold them. She asked if they would run space heaters for the bedrooms in the *dawdi haus* because she wouldn't have time to chop wood and care for Michael too.

"I just thought of something," I said. "Since Michael's home care person isn't coming now, I'll be glad to look in on him while you're working."

Isaac steered our other horse, Sadie, from the barn. She was pulling the wagon while Nick was tied to the back. He waved. "See you later, *Bruder*. Goodbye, Joanna. It was nice to meet you."

As the wagon rattled down our driveway, Joanna touched my sleeve again. "You are so sweet to offer to help with Michael, Jared." She stood on tip toe. Just when I thought she was going to kiss me, she squeezed my nose. "Merry Christmas, Rudolf."

Grinning, she dropped to her heels, and I rubbed my nose. "Who's Rudolf, and what's he got to do with you pinching my nose?"

"Rudolf the Red-Nosed Reindeer is a TV Christmas classic. I thought if I pinched your nose, it would get red, and I'd call you Rudolf."

I stopped rubbing my nose. "Why am I glad us Amish don't watch television?"

"I don't know, Rudolf. As much as I'm going to teach you about the English way of celebrating Christmas, it's too bad you haven't watched TV."

I walked her to the rental car. She got in and rolled the window down. "See you next Saturday, Rudolf."

The little car puttered to life. Joanna rolled the window up and drove away, leaving me to rub my wrinkled forehead. What an interesting woman she was—fun to be with, a fine sister to her sick *bruder*, and too cute for comfort.

Instead of rubbing my forehead, I should've slapped it. Not only was it time to find out Susan's intentions toward our marriage, it was time to find out her intentions toward Jacob Graber.

In the house at the table, I left a note telling Isaac I was going to see Susan. Bishop Bontrager had let our community vote on the use of bicycles last year. Since it was only a mile to Susan's, I got my bike from the barn and headed down the road.

Five minutes later, I parked in front of Susan's house and knocked on the door. At least Jacob Graber wasn't here to interfere.

Sarah came to the screen door, wiping her hands with a dish towel. "*Willkumme*, Jared. If you're here for Susan, she's feeding the chickens."

I thanked Sarah and left for the henhouse, behind the huge, red barn. Standing outside it, tossing feed in the yard, Susan looked up. "Oh, Jared. What a surprise."

I removed my straw hat. "I was hoping you could tell me about Jacob Graber."

"What about him?"

"About him coming to supper the other night."

"*Daed* invited him, remember?" A slight grin played at the corners of Susan's mouth. "Look at you, jealous of Jacob and me. You know better than that."

"I'm not jealous," I said, flustered. "It just seemed you and your folks preferred him over me. We didn't even take a buggy ride to talk about our engagement. Have you told your folks yet?"

Susan threw more chicken feed. "I'm keeping it to myself until we set a wedding date. I was hoping we could get married near Christmas." She looked away and back, as if something were troubling her. "I'm glad you came. I've been wanting to apologize for wanting to kiss, and, well, other things. It was very wrong to suggest those things until we're husband and wife."

The sincerity in her voice made me believe her. Perhaps we'd make a good match after all. "Well, I suppose young folks like us think about those things."

"I'm glad you admit it, Jared. What do you think of getting married near Christmas? I think it would be a good way for a forgetful man to remember our anniversary."

Susan's smile said she was teasing. "I suppose it's possible," I said. "We'll discuss it again the closer it gets to November. If your folks agree, Bishop Bontrager should agree." No sooner than I said those words, a vision of Joanna calling me Rudolph after pinching my nose appeared. It seemed *Gott* was trying to tell me something. Since she was *Englisch* and we couldn't marry, what could it be?

Susan threw the chickens a last handful of feed and grasped my hand. "I look forward to starting our lives together. I think we'll be a fine match."

I agreed and said I better get home. As I pedaled along the road, Susan's last words puzzled me. Wasn't she supposed to know we were a fine match instead of just thinking it? I could be reading too much into her statement, but it was still worthy of consideration. If she had any doubts about marrying me, especially since I had doubts of my own, she should admit them.

I glanced up into the sky. *Gott, what a hypocrite I am, not admitting my doubts to Susan like I say she should admit hers to me. I'm not sure what you have planned for us, but I hope we figure it out sooner than later. The last thing we need is a marriage with secrets. Amen.*

Chapter 8

Joanna

People often say it's strange how time flies. I agree, except it seems to fly a lot faster when I'm busy, and I've been extremely busy since May.

Jared and Isaac helped move mine and Michael's furniture into the *dawdi haus*. I was going to let the new owners keep the stove and refrigerator. When I asked them about it, they said to take them if I wanted because they were going to get new ones. Since the stove was propane, it would fit right into my new, sort of, Amish lifestyle.

As anyone who's moved knows, there's more to it than simply moving stuff. A month after Michael and I were settled, I bought a propane generator large enough to power the entire house.

Someone might ask how I could do that with my money problems. The answer was my rent was way less than the house payment had been, and I'd gotten a nice raise at work. Isn't God good?

Another way the move was complicated —well, after the move was over and I'd bought the generator—was by hiring an electrician to wire the entire house. Because of Michael's lack of mobility and the necessity of warm soap and water, Bishop Bontrager graciously allowed me to hire a plumber for running water, a water heater, a bathroom, and a kitchen sink. "After all," he said, offering me a soft smile, "you're not Amish, and it wouldn't be kind to force our ways on you."

I'd driven to his home, and we were

sitting on his porch swing. Returning his smile, I thanked him. As I started to leave, a curious thought kept me seated. "Bishop, except for before my parents died and Michael got sick, I don't think I've ever been this happy. I've always believed in living simply and being grateful for every blessing. Since the Amish live like that, I guess that's what it is."

In the June heat, a female bluebird flew to the oak shading the porch. The bishop's eyes followed it before coming to me again. "Cherish your feelings, Joanna. Whether we're Amish or not, those who are truly grateful treasure the simple things in life."

A male bluebird joined his mate. They began warbling to each other, then flew away, two streaks of blue against an even bluer sky.

"I see you watching them," the bishop said. "When we spoke about you moving to our community, you said you didn't have a special young man in your life. Do those bluebirds give you any regrets?"

The only regret I had was how I'd acted toward Jared during our picnic. If we were meant to be together, as I'd thought at the time, how could that be when I would never be Amish and he'd never be English?

"Ah," Bishop Bontrager said. "Those wrinkles on your forehead say my question has you seriously considering it. Do you have someone in mind?"

"Not really," I said, regretting my dishonesty. "The only thing I want is to make Michael's last months happy months."

The bishop's expression softened. "If I might ask, what are your plans for his funeral?"

I had thought about it, but actually speaking with someone about it brought tears to my eyes. I fingered them away before answering. "Our parents are buried in our church cemetery. I haven't asked Michael what he wants. I guess he'll be okay with that."

"The most important thing is for him to he feel at home," the bishop said. "Since you both feel at home in our community, I could ask everyone at our next church service if they would allow him into our cemetery."

My eyes widened. "I didn't think the Amish allowed a non-Amish person to be buried in their cemetery."

"Most don't. Our community formed to worship freely instead of being constrained by the words of men. The New Testament couldn't be clearer concerning this. Although we follow most Amish doctrine, we make allowances as we see fit. Would you like me to ask them?"

The kindness and understanding of this man warmed my heart, and his words made me feel even more at home than at my own church. I'd visited it once a week, but only to see my parents' graves. The people there were nice, the minister too, so why did I feel more at home in this community, especially with it being Amish?

I told the bishop he could ask, but Michael would have the final decision.

At home again, I found him in what had become his favorite place, in the shade of the *dawdi haus's* porch, a serene smile on his face, and I understood completely.

We'd begun this ritual on the first Saturday morning after we'd moved in, me in a rocking chair, Michael in his wheelchair, us sharing sips of after-breakfast coffee from the same cup. In the field before us, holding the reins of two horses, Isaac steered a cultivator between rows of half-grown corn. We loved the smell of freshly turned earth, the metallic clang of a stone occasionally striking the curved tines, Isaac's booming voice as he said, "Good horses, good horses."

On this particular morning, Jared had welcomed us by bringing a breakfast of oatmeal pancakes and crispy bacon, then leaving to let us enjoy it alone. I admired him for this because he knew how close Michael and I were. Unfortunately, that afternoon, mine and Michael's peace was interrupted by Susan Yoder, Jared's fiancé.

We'd eaten supper and were back on the porch. In the twilight, Jared and Isaac were drawing water from the well to heat for their baths. I'd already bathed Michael, and I'd do the same for myself after I got him in bed.

As far as Susan, when someone is driving a wagon along a driveway—the horse snorting, its hooves stomping, the driver's kapp halfway off her head, her pinned red hair coming loose—that someone gets your attention.

Nearing the porch, she jerked the reins, set the wagon's brake, and jumped to the ground to climb the steps. "Are you Joanna Weaver?"

From Michael's wheelchair, he looked up. "Who you? Why you mad?"

"I'm engaged to Jared. That's who I am."

Michael cut his eyes at me. "Uh-oh."

"What's wrong?" I asked Susan.

She slapped her hands to her hips "'What's wrong?' she asked, mocking me sarcastically. "What's wrong is I just found out about you. That's what's wrong."

"I'm not in control of who tells you about me," I said. "Besides, you act like I mean more to Jared than I do. Did the person who told you about me tell you all I am is the person renting this house? If not, they should have."

Susan's cheeked flared redder than the setting sun over the horizon. "It doesn't matter what someone told me. An Amish man shouldn't have a single woman living close enough to tempt him."

I glared up at her. "In case you can't tell by my lack of Pennsylvania Dutch accent and my car you parked your wagon behind, I'm not Amish, so I'm the last person on earth to tempt Jared into anything."

The screen door of the house next door

squeaked open, and Jared hurried over. "What in the world is going on, Susan? I could hear you yelling in my bedroom."

Susan shot a shaking fingertip at me. "Why must I find out about her from Jacob instead of you? We're engaged. Engaged people don't lie to each other."

"Uh-oh," Michael said again, tempting me to laugh."

"What's so funny?" Susan demanded.

"You are," Michael said, giving her a lopsided grin.

Jared took hold of Susan's arm. "I just haven't told you yet."

She snatched her arm away. "Jacob said you offered her the *dawdi haus* last month. That's plenty of time to tell me."

"Why are you so upset?" Jared waved a hand toward Michael and I. "Look how calm Joanna and Michael are. They're behaving more Amish than you are, coming here with jealousy and accusations."

I nodded. "If anyone has a right to be

jealous, I'd say it's Jared. Whoever Jacob is, he sure likes stirring up trouble. Is he doing that to break you and Jared up because he wants you?"

Susan's creamy complexion, not quite as white as snow, turned even whiter. "I ... he ... we— No, not at all. He's just concerned. That's all."

Jared's flaring nostrils said otherwise. He took Susan by the elbow and led her to the buggy. "It's time to tell the truth. Do you want me or do you want Jacob?"

"Oh!" Susan huffed. "Now you blame me for your cheating? How dare you!"

"Uh-oh," Michael said a third time.

Although I was tempted to laugh again, I didn't like causing this argument between Jared and Susan. Yes, I cared about him, and if I'd been Amish, I'd court him in a heartbeat. That wasn't going to happen, so I joined him and Susan at the wagon. "I'm sorry about this," I told Susan, "but since I'm not Amish, why are you so jealous? It's not like Jared and I can ever court or marry." I smiled up at Jared. "Jared's a great guy. As far as your friend Jacob, great guys don't try to break up a couple unless he has feelings for the woman. Is that how it is?"

Jared crossed his arms. "Or unless the woman has feelings for the man. Is that how it is, too?"

Isaac, his hair wet and his suspenders hanging loose, came out on his porch barefooted, a cell phone in hand. "Jared, Jacob wants to know if Susan is here."

Jared shook his head. "See what Jacob has done, Susan? Now he has us using our phone for personal calls instead of business calls." He went to Isaac for the phone and took it to Susan. "Go ahead. Tell him you're here." He started to give Susan the phone, then raised it to his ear. "Jacob, this is Jared. If you want Susan enough to cause all this trouble, you can have her." He slipped the phone into his pocket. "Are you happy now, Susan? He's who you wanted anyway, isn't he?"

"You don't love me, Jared. You never showed it at all."

Her revelation shocked me. Jared was kind and considerate, so she must've meant he hadn't showed his love in physical ways. From the few boyfriends I'd had, I'd quickly learned they felt the same, and I wanted no part of a relationship like that.

Jared shook his head, his blonde curls reminding me of an angry lion. He pointed at the wagon. "The wedding is off. If you and Jacob start spreading rumors about Joanna and me —"

"We'll all tell Bishop Bontrager," Isaac said, still on the porch.

"Me too," Michael said from his wheelchair.

After Susan climbed into the wagon, Jared looked up at her. "For what it's worth, I hope you and Jacob are happy. The more I've thought about it, the more I doubted our marriage. When you see him, tell him I said *denke*."

Without a word or a glance, Susan snapped the horse's reins. Soon it was clip-clopping along the highway.

Watching Susan leave, Jared turned to face me. "I apologize. You've done nothing to deserve her ridiculous accusations."

Isaac left the porch to join us. "*Bruder*, count your blessings. You weren't sure about marrying Susan, and you were right."

Jared gave him the phone. "I suppose so. It's too bad I didn't know that before I proposed."

"She said someone called Jacob told her," I said. "Who is he?"

"A young man in the community," Jared said. "I suppose Bishop Bontrager mentioned you moving here to someone, and word got out. People were going to find out eventually, so it doesn't matter how Susan knows."

"Jo-yanna," Michael said, his voice barely a whisper. Fear knotted my throat.

He sounded weaker than I'd ever heard.

I rushed to him, Jared and Isaac on my heels. "What is it?" I asked, searching his face for signs of him leaving me.

"I tired. Go bed, okay?"

Icy relief flooded my veins. "Sure, Michael." He'd been getting weaker lately, so I pushed his chair toward the door before he could use the electric wheelchair's joystick.

Jared opened the door. Isaac said he was going to finish bathing. Jared followed me inside to Michael's room and knelt to look him in the eye. "Michael, I'll help get you ready for bed if you don't mind."

Michael gave a weak nod. "It ok, Ja-wed."

I asked Michael if he needed a new diaper, and he shook his head. "Just sleep."

Jared faced me. "How do you help him get ready for bed?"

"I slip my hands under his arms and wrap my arms around his back, like a hug.

Then I pick him up and sit him on the bed."
I faced Michael. "I forgot to brush your
teeth." I rolled him to the bathroom. Done
in there, ending with him rinsing and
spitting into a bowl, I rolled him back to the
bed.

Jared had already pulled the covers
back. He went to Michael. "Are you ready?"

"Weady, Ja-wed."

Jared picked him up like I'd described
and sat him on the bed. I took his shoes and
shirt off and worked a T-shirt over his thin
arms. Jared and I eased his head to the
pillow. Then we took his socks and pants off
and put his pajama bottoms on. I'd put a
battery operated fan on the nightstand to
help with the June heat, so the sheet would
do to cover him. I leaned over to kiss my
sweet brother's cheek. "See you in the
morning."

After Michael nodded slowly, his eyes
focused on Jared. "You good man, Ja-wed.
You need good woman like Jo-yanna."

Jared patted Michael's hand on his stomach. "You're a better man than me, Michael. I'm sure your faith is helping you through this trial. You're an inspiration to me."

Jared told Michael goodnight, and I closed the door behind us. In the kitchen, as Jared was leaving, I grabbed his arm to turn him around. "I'm sorry about Susan. You were right to doubt her."

Sadness filled Jared's blue eyes. He brushed a tear from one cheek. "I cared about her, but marriage is something very different. I've never been in love, so I'm not sure how that feels. Have you ever been in love?"

The need to lie about my feelings tugged at my heart. Every time I turned around, Jared was kind, helpful, and gentle. Still, we couldn't be together, so I decided on a version of the truth from before my parents moved. "I met a guy once. He was kind, helpful, and gentle."

Jared's cheek twitched, as if my loving someone else bothered him. "Can I ask what happened?"

"We were only three or four. In fact, he's one of my first memories." I stepped close and tousled Jared's hair. "Your curls remind me of him."

Jared smiled, embarrassment in his pink cheeks. "I meant when you were older, Joanna."

"Enough about me," I said firmly. "Have you liked anyone besides Susan?"

"I told you how my parents' illnesses kept Isaac and me from courting. I liked a couple, but she's the first girl I was seriously interested in."

My pursing lips twisted into a smile. "What about the second girl you were interested in? Didn't you tell me about her?"

Like a plowed field, a row of wrinkles furrowed Jared's brow. "I never told you about anyone like that."

I poked his stomach. "I mean me, silly. If

you hadn't liked me, you wouldn't have taken me on a buggy ride and picnic."

"Oh, that," Jared said, humor in his voice. "She was okay, but I thought her *bruder* needed a picnic more than she did. I would if I were him because he has to put up with his teasing *schwester*."

Through the screen door and from the road, the clip-clop of a horse's hooves echoed in the darkening night. They slowed and changed to the thud of horseshoes on a dirt drive, coming closer and closer. I followed Jared to the porch. "It's late for visitors, " he said. "I wonder who it is."

A pair of lights brightened the front of the buggy, so we couldn't tell who was inside. It parked behind my car, and Susan climbed down. "Jared, can we please talk?"

He crossed the yard to her. "What is it?"

"I'm sorry about what happened. I don't want Jacob. Can you please forgive me?"

Jared raked a hand through his hair. "I don't know. After what you said and did, especially since you and Jacob seem to have something going on … well, I don't know."

"What if we just court again? We don't have to be engaged. Then later, if we're both sure, we can get married."

"Susan, I don't think—"

"I know it's my fault," she sobbed. "I was afraid I might lose you. That's why I wanted to do more than kiss. Please say you'll give us another chance."

She fell against Jared's chest, and I felt a surge of sympathy for him. It seemed Susan really did love him, and he had to decide if he wanted to salvage their relationship. The selfish part of me hoped he would send her on her way, while the sympathetic part understood how she felt because I'd felt the same way when Jared refused to consider us having a relationship.

Jared held her at arm's length. "What about Jacob? What's going on between you two?"

"I made him think I liked him to make

you jealous. I just came from his house and admitted it. He forgave me. If he can, you can."

Even with night falling, I could see anger twisting Jared's face, illuminated by the buggy's lights. "You lied to him about your feelings to make me jealous." Jared took a step backward. "You took your vows. You promised to follow our community's *Ordnung*." He gestured toward me. "See Joanna on the porch? Her *bruder* has a terrible disease. Some people might lose faith because of it. Instead of doing that, she is as good to him as if she were his *mamm*."

"But I lied because I love you," Susan wailed. "Doesn't that mean anything to you?"

"You seem to be forgetting everything that makes us Amish, Susan. One of those things is not discussing private matters out in the open." He pointed at the buggy. "Go home. We need a few days apart to clear our heads. We'll talk after the church service next Sunday."

Susan's trembling hand reached for Jared's hand. If he let her take it, I'd lose him forever.

He let her take it.

"You … you really mean it?" she asked. "You'll give me another chance?"

"I can't promise," Jared said, his voice still firm. "We'll have to see how it goes."

Susan released his hand and climbed into the buggy. "You'll see. It'll go well, and we'll be married next year at Christmas."

As she left, Jared joined me again on the porch. "I apologize, Joanna. No one should have to witness a scene like that."

Sorrow that I'd lost him filled me with dread. Despite our differences, his character at forgiving Susan and his willingness to help me with Michael were confirming what I'd thought for a while now—I could marry this fine man and be happy for the rest of my life. If there was a chance of it happening, I didn't know how. All I could do was to keep my faith that God would provide a miracle, and for me to recognize it if—or when—it happened.

Chapter 9

Jared

Jah, I'd been disappointed in Susan for wanting me to kiss her, and especially for the other things she'd suggested. Regardless, using Jacob to make me jealous, and even more-so, to accuse Joanna like she did, disappointed me past my limit. Still, *Gott* wants us to forgive, so when Susan seemed sincere with her apology, that's what I did.

In all honesty though, before then, when I said Jacob could have her, a spark of hope had flared in my mind. If I weren't engaged, and if *Gott* provided a miracle to allow Joanna and me to be together, I'd be forever grateful.

After I met Susan to discuss our relationship, I returned home to tell Isaac. Although he admired me for forgiving her, he didn't for giving her the hope of a possible marriage. He'd picked up the habit of rubbing his nose when he was frustrated, and did so then. "What are you thinking, *Bruder*? You don't love her, *jah*?"

"How do I know?" I replied. "I've never been in love."

Sitting at the kitchen table with farm paperwork, he frowned. "Believe me, you'll know it when it happens."

Not wanting to pry into his personal life, I didn't ask how he knew until the day before Thanksgiving, when I had more evidence of his answer.

All that summer, claiming to need a buggy ride to relax after each week of work, he would hitch Sadie to the courting buggy and leave for two hours or more every Sunday afternoon. When I combined his rides with him sitting across from Fanny Bontrager during our youth singings, plus speaking with her more and more after each volleyball game, I knew my *bruder* was courting.

Then came the week of Thanksgiving. Our community held weddings starting in October and going through March. Since he and Fanny hadn't married yet, I wanted to know if they would anytime soon. Otherwise, we couldn't make plans for them living in our house.

It was the morning before Thanksgiving. As a fine snow fell, Isaac and I were making desserts for the community meal. I liked our *mamm's* recipe for pumpkin pie, with just a bit more cinnamon than most people preferred. Isaac liked her recipe for apple fritter bread, also with more cinnamon than most people preferred. As everyone knew, we loved our cinnamon. We'd already roasted a turkey and made dressing for ourselves at home. With all the fine cooks in our community, the table tomorrow would be filled with plenty of roasted turkeys and baked hams, along with various rolls, vegetables, and casseroles. Counting cakes, pies, cookies, and other desserts, it would be a memorable day for eating.

I'd taken my pies from the oven and had placed them on the table to cool. Every few minutes, Jared peeked into the oven, concerned with removing his bread at just the right moment. When he finally brought his pans to the table to cool, I asked him to sit so I could ask him something. As he did, his blue eyes took on a humorous glint. "I wouldn't mind," he said, "but our Ordnung doesn't allow it. Maybe Bishop Bontrager can get everyone to make an allowance for you and Joanna."

I tilted my head to one side. "You wouldn't mind what?"

"If you married Joanna. She's a fine

person, much more sincere than Susan."

I waved his joke away. "That's impossible and you know it. Now, what *is* possible is you marrying Fanny Bontrager."

Isaac's eyebrows twitched upward. "I have no idea what you're talking about." He broke out into a smile. "It wondered me how long it would be before you asked. Did my talking to her after volleyball give us away?"

"And singing with her. And your Sunday rides in the courting buggy." I smirked at him. "I'm not as dumb as you look, you know."

Isaac chuckled. "If that were the case, we'd both look dumb because we're twins. Yes, Fanny and I are engaged. Do you mind if we live here? After all, your future wife lives in the *dawdi haus*."

"You and your joking," I said. "I'm happy for you and Fanny. It'll be nice to have some nieces and nephews running around the farm."

"What about you and Susan? Are you going to court her again? I wouldn't. As dishonest as she was about wanting to make you jealous by using Jacob, you can't trust her."

I told my *bruder* I agreed. "I suppose, though, if she were afraid of losing me like she said, I understand … to a degree, I mean."

"But not to the degree of courting her again?" Isaac asked.

"I'm not sure. I don't care for her doubting me even though it was justified. If we marry, her doubts should end, and we might fall in love like *Gott* intends for married couples.

Isaac drummed his fingertips on the table. "The happiest marriages are with couples who love each other before the wedding, *Bruder*, not after. I know because Fanny and I love each other very much."

We had the window above the basin opened a little to let the heat from the wood stove out. Through it came the sound of a vehicle engine coming closer in the driveway. I looked at Isaac. "Are you expecting anyone?"

Without answering, he got up to look out the window in the door. "It's a man in one of those vehicles the *Englisch* call an SUV. He parked at the *dawdi haus* and is getting out."

As I heard the man close the SUV door, Isaac got a mug from the cabinet. He asked if I wanted coffee, and I said no. He filled the mug at the wood stove and returned to the table.

Minutes later, visible through the door window, Joanna, wearing a red jacket, snowflakes dotting her hair, knocked. When I waved her in, Isaac offered her coffee. "No thank you," she said. "I was hoping for a favor. The owner of my old house has some heavy boxes he found in the attic. "Do you mind helping me take them in so he doesn't have to stay?"

I appreciated Joanna's thoughtfulness. "I'll be there after I get my coat and hat on."

Isaac swallowed coffee. "My *bruder* is a kind fellow, isn't he?"

"Kind enough to not need your help." I took my black felt hat from the rack by the door and put it on. "Are you kind enough to fetch water and heat it so we can wash our dishes?"

He raised the cup. "Right after I finish my coffee."

I donned my coat and followed Joanna to the SUV. The driver raised the rear door, climbed back inside, and I didn't blame him. The inside of the SUV was much warmer than the freezing wind that was now swirling the snow about.

There were four cardboard boxes, the flaps taped down. They were more large than heavy, so it took both Joanna and I to carry them up her porch steps and inside. When we were through, she thanked the man, closed the rear door of the SUV, and tramped through the deepening snow to the house. "Come on in and have some hot chocolate," she said, holding the door open.

At the door, I stamped snow from my boots and went inside. On the wall by the door, my hat and coat joined Joanna's coat. Near a space heater, Michael, in his wheelchair, a book propped on a holder attached to the tray, looked up at me. "He-wo, Ja-wed. See snow?"

"I did," I said. "It's coming down pretty well now."

"I like snow ... like Chri-mas. You?"

I assumed he meant he liked snow for Christmas. "I do too. It doesn't seem like Christmas without snow."

Joanna took a mug of steaming milk from the microwave. She tore a packet open, stirred the contents into the milk, inserted a straw into it and placed the mug on Michael's tray. "There you go. Let it cool first."

"Okay, Jo-yanna."

Done with two more mugs, she took them to the table, where we sat across from each other and sipped.

"Mmm, this is good," I said, lowering the mug. "I never tried hot chocolate from a little packet. Isaac and I make ours with cocoa and sugar."

Joanna licked the dark stain from her lips. "The grocery store has it. It's dark chocolate flavor."

Her brown hair, which had barely reached the nape of her neck when we met, now reached the collar of her red sweater. "I see your hair is growing."

She ran her fingers through it. "My mousy brown mess. I just brush it and let it go."

I was curious about the boxes we'd stacked by the refrigerator. "How old are those clothes?"

"Old enough for me to not remember them." Joanna raised the mug and sipped. "My parents never mentioned putting anything in the attic." She got up and raised one of the flaps until the tape stopped her. "I think they're old clothes. I'll slide the boxes in the spare bedroom and check them later. If we can't use the clothes, I'll give them to the needy."

I closed my eyes for a count of three. Yet again, Joanna had shown me another reason to admire her, this time with her willingness to help others.

She reached across the table to touch my hand. "You seem to have something on your mind. Is it Susan? I've been wondering if you'll court her again."

Her touch warmed my hand like a spring rain. What was wrong with me? Why did I keep torturing myself with thoughts of her? I swallowed to steady myself. "Isaac and I were talking about marriage. He said the happiest marriages are with couples who love each other before the wedding."

"Ah, and that struck a nerve because you're not sure if you love Susan." Joanna ran a fingertip around the rim of the mug. "Isaac's a smart man."

"He's a blessed man, too," I said. "He proposed to Bishop Bontrager's daughter Fanny. He says they're in love, so I'm sure they'll be a fine match."

Joanna stopped fingering the mug. "Do you ever think …" Her lips pressed together. "I shouldn't say."

"We're friends," I told her. "You can ask me anything."

She glanced at Michael, as if she didn't want him to hear us. Thankfully, he was busy with his hot chocolate. Facing me again, she continued. "Do you ever think about what you told me at our picnic?"

How could I not think about it? I thought about it every time I saw her, but I couldn't tell her that.

"Jared?"

"*Jah?*"

"Do you?"

"I suppose you mean when I said it feels

like *Gott* brought you into my life for a reason."

"Yes. Do you think about it?"

"I ..."

"Does it hurt that much to admit it?"

I blinked until a single tear rolled down my cheek. "It hurts every time I see you because we can't be together."

"I see," Joanna said, her voice barely above a whisper. "I don't like hurting you. Should Michael and I move?"

Wiping that single tear away, I squared my shoulders. "I'll get over my feelings eventually. What's important is you and Michael having a home. I wouldn't feel right if you left because of me."

Joanna's lower lip trembled. "Jared, if you think I'm in love with you, I'm not. I think of you as a friend, so maybe that'll help you get over your feelings for me."

I knew she was lying to protect me. I could see the truth in her brown eyes, could hear it in her quavering voice, could sense it in the very air around us. We were in love, and there was absolutely nothing we could do to stop the thunderstorm of anguish that was blowing our way. How could that be when I firmly believed *Gott* had brought us together for a purpose?

Joanna was looking down into her mug. I closed my eyes. *Dear Gott, I've been faithful ever since I came to know your holy Son, Jesus, and I pray that I'll eventually understand your plans for Joanna and I. Amen.*

When I opened my eyes, Joanna was watching me intently. "You were praying, weren't you? I was too, praying that I'd stop hurting you."

A sudden calm surrounded me, similar to the sunny day of our picnic, when we walked while holding hands. I reached across the table to take her hand in mine. "Please don't worry about me. I think *Gott* just took my pain away."

Like a butterfly's wings as it fluttered around a sunflower, Joanna blinked again and again. "Are you sure?"

I nodded. "Do you believe in miracles?"

"After Michael's diagnosis and losing our parents, you'd think I wouldn't, but I do. Do you see one in our future?"

Since we couldn't marry, I didn't want to give Joanna false hope. "I see one in our present. *Gott* took my pain away, so we can be friends now. I hope that's all right with you. Is it?"

"Well, It's not like I'll become Amish or you'll become English, so that's the best we can do."

Relieved at the progress we'd made with our feelings, I stood to go. "I'm glad. That means I can cut a cedar for your Christmas tree. Then you can teach me how to decorate it."

Chapter 10

Joanna

Having fed Michael his breakfast, I set an MP3 player on his wheelchair table. Although he could still turn the pages of a book, we agreed it would be much easier for him to listen to audiobooks. I kissed his cheek and started an Amish Christmas novel I'd recently bought. In the kitchen, I washed our dishes while waiting for Jared. It was the Saturday before Christmas, and a beautiful snow had blanketed the world overnight. I'd mentioned the chance of snow yesterday, when we made plans to cut my tree, but he promised to take me anyway.

Regardless of the conversation concerning our feelings, I was finding it harder and harder to deny them. Still, for Jared's sake, since he might decide to court Susan at any time, I kept them to myself. If there was one thing I wanted for him, it was for him to be happy, even if that happened by courting and marrying Susan.

A horse's whinny caught my attention. I looked out the window over the sink. Jared was leading Nick from the pasture to the barn. I donned my thickest coat, a red stocking hat, and insulated gloves. I already wore a pair of winter boots to ward off the freezing cold, evidenced by the thermometer outside the kitchen window that said it was twenty-degrees.

I told Michael we'd be back soon and opened the door to a blast of frigid air. As I walked through the crunching snow to the barn, my breath clouded the air before my face.

When I reached the open double doors, Jared was climbing into the wagon's seat. "Ah, I was just coming to get you."

After I climbed in beside him, he clucked his tongue to urge Nick outside. "Do you have a tree in mind?" I asked.

The wide-brimmed felt hat shadowed his face, cheeks growing pink from the cold. "Do you like surprises?"

"Good ones," I said. "Will this be a good one?"

He beamed a smile at me. "Always for you, Joanna."

He steered Nick behind the barn, toward the rear of the farm. In the fields flanking the road, corn stubble poked above the snow. Boot prints, both coming and going, marked the road, making me curious. "Did you come out here?" I asked. "The snow last night would've covered those boot prints."

Jared's gloved hands tugged the reins, steering Nick around a curve in the road. "I made sure the snow hadn't broken any branches on your tree this morning. I want it to be perfect for you and Michael."

His expression softened, and I heard his unspoken words—*I want it to be perfect for you and Michael because this might be your last Christmas together.*

This thought both saddened and strengthened me. The last thing I wanted was to lose Michael, but his attitude toward death, filled with his faith of going to Heaven to see our parents, calmed my soul more than anything I could think of.

The fields ended at a creek gurgling over a bed of rounded stones and began again on the other side. We crossed a bridge made of hand-hewn wooden posts, supporting logs that were sawed in half. Nick started up a small rise. When we topped it, Jared pointed to the left. "I hope coming to our picnic spot is all right. The best tree I could find is on an old fence row to the left of that little clearing."

I shaded my eyes from the sun reflecting off the snow. "I don't see a fence."

"It's inside the woods. There's an old home place marked by a stone foundation. It's in a small clearing that lets the sun shine through. If not, the tree wouldn't have filled out so well."

He steered Nick along the left side of the small field, parked and set the wagon's brake. At the back, after getting a cross-cut saw, he started toward the woods, me at his side.

The crisp air, fresher than any spring breeze, burned my sinuses. As clouds of white puffed from my nose, I shoved my gloved hands into my coat pockets. Jared glanced my way. "We'll warm up when we start sawing the tree."

I gave him a teasing grin. "You mean I have to saw, too?"

Instead of answering, he continued into the woods, eventually stopping to point. "See how the snow is raised to form a rectangle? That's the foundation of the old house. Beyond it is your—"

"That's my tree?" I asked, amazed at its size. "It'll fit in the barn, but not in my house."

Jared chuckled. "You're not much of a farm girl. We'll use the upper half."

He led me to the tree. Beside it, I looked up into its branches. "It's a shame to cut it." I pointed. "See the bird nest?"

Jared also pointed. "There's a squirrel nest, too. I didn't see that before." He lowered his hand. "I found a few smaller trees, if you'd rather get one of those."

I looked up into Jared's blue eyes, my love for him impossible to deny. "You are so sweet, caring, and kind, Jared. If you marry Susan, I hope she appreciates you."

Several white breaths clouded his face before he answered. "I've never thought about this. She's never said anything about me being sweet, or caring, or kind."

"I remember," I said. "You said she

seemed to only appreciate your looks."

He dropped the saw. "Why haven't I thought of that? It's important for someone who says they love you to think those things about you."

"I didn't mean to make you doubt her," I said, picking up the saw and giving it to him. "Let's find my tree and get it home. Then we'll have the rest of the morning to decorate it."

The remainder of our outing was fairly quiet. I approved the second tree Jared showed me. He also cut a small tree for his and Isaac's and Fanny's table, as they'd been married since the second Tuesday in December. All three had invited me to the wedding. Thankfully I had to work. The last thing I wanted was to face Susan again after our confrontation.

Jared also gathered some evergreen branches, saying they would be decorated with ribbon, put in baskets, and placed in the windows. Thinking the Amish didn't use Christmas trees, I asked about the small tree for the table, and he said the community had gotten permission from Bishop Bontrager.

At home again, Jared and I sawed the tree to length in the wagon. Then we took it inside and secured it in the holder I'd brought from the other house. Done placing it in a corner of the living area, I watered it and asked Michael what he thought. In typical Michael humor, he gave it a thumbs up. "Ve-wy nice, Yo-anna. Tank you, Ja-wed."

"Okay," I said, eyeing the tree, "I better get out the decorations."

Jared followed me to the extra bedroom, where much of mine and Michael's stuff was still packed from the move. He went to the boxes he'd helped bring in. "I see you haven't gone through these clothes yet."

I gave him two boxes of red, gold, and green glass balls and two boxes of ornaments shaped like stars. "No criticizing my junk room, Mr. Lapp." He studied the stars through the cellophane window in the box. "We hang stars like these around the house for Christmas."

"How about that," I said, leaning over to take two more boxes of ornaments from the same cardboard box. "Something else we have in common."

"We do have a lot in common, don't we?"

"Uh-huh, like how we both love Christmas." I showed him the ornaments. "Look, they're little snowballs. I'd put lights on the tree, but I don't want to strain the generator."

By the tree again, I showed Jared how to hang everything around it for variety. With his help, it didn't take long to finish.

"Uh-oh," Michael said. "You for-got angel."

I snapped my fingers. "I sure did. Be right back." I left for the angel, found it beneath some old tinsel in the same box, and joined Jared and Michael again.

"Let Ja-wed do it," Michael said.

I showed Jared the bottom of the angel. "See that place beneath her dress? Just slide that over the top of the tree."

Jared went to Michael and knelt by his wheelchair. "I can hold you up if you want to put it on."

Michael faced me. "Do it same time. You and Ja-wed. Make this Christ—" The Adam's apple in his thin neck bobbed with a hard swallow. "Make this Christmas special."

I held in a sob. Michael knew he might not live to see another Christmas. He also seemed to know I cared deeply for Jared, and it would make my sweet brother happier to see Jared and I put the angel on the tree than him putting it on.

"All right," Jared said, joining me at the tree. As I held the angel with my right hand, Jared held it with his left hand, and we raised it to the top of the tree.

"Yay!" Michael said. "Tank you. Now this Christmas special."

Jared smiled at the tree, then faced Michael. "My Christmas is special because you and Joanna came into my life. You two aren't Amish, but I'd do anything for you like I would my Amish *bruders* and *schwesters*."

Michael slowly raised a hand to point at the tree. "Mistletoe, Yo-anna. Kiss Jared for tree."

"There's no mistletoe in that tree," Jared said. "Besides, I enjoyed getting it for you."

"It in bottom."

I peered into the thick branches, fragrant with the smell of cedar, then pulled out a clump of mistletoe and shook it at my sneaky brother. "This is plastic. You got it out of the boxes while we were cutting the tree, didn't you?"

Michael shrugged. "Not me. I good, like angel."

Jared sputtered laughter. "That crooked

grin says you're no angel." He faced me and whispered, "It's all right. Anything to make him happy."

What can a loving sister do but make her brother happy? I raised the mistletoe over Jared's head, and he leaned down to give me a quick kiss."

"That no kiss," Michael said, his tone critical.

While Jared's cheeks turned as red as several of the glass balls on the tree, I stood on tiptoe. "Pucker up. You're getting a proper kiss whether you want it or not."

Jared leaned down again, this time kissing me to a count of five, leaving me a bit swimmy headed when I dropped to my heels.

"Much better," Michael said, again grinning his crooked grin. "Time for hot chocolate."

Luckily for Jared and I, my sneaky brother didn't make us kiss any more. We did enjoy the rest of the afternoon, though.

Along with the hot chocolate, we had peanut butter cookies I'd baked and listened to some of Michael's book with him.

Except for roast beef and all the trimmings, because Michael and I were tired of turkey from our recent Thanksgiving meal, that was pretty much our Christmas, and I was grateful that the good Lord saw fit to allow Michael to experience it.

Unfortunately for my gratitude, that Christmas left me with two nagging worries. One was how many more days, weeks, and months it would be until ALS claimed my sweet brother. The other worry was how many more days, weeks, and months it would be before Susan claimed my sweet Jared.

Whenever those worries interrupted work or my time with Michael, my faith would grip me with conviction, and that still, small voice the faithful experience would say things will work out as God would have it, not that I would have it.

This conviction carried me through January. When an overnight blizzard covered my immediate world in two feet of snow, stranding myself and my co-workers at home, my boss's four-wheel drive SUV came to the rescue.

It carried me through February. When Michael and I were in bed with the flu, Fanny brought steaming tea and vegetable soup.

It carried me through March. When Michael's doctor told me his new symptoms—the difficulty swallowing and the difficulty breathing—meant he would need palliative care by a hospice worker before Easter, I prayed and prayed and prayed for God to share His strength with me like He was sharing it with Michael.

Then, three days before Easter, after the hospice worker had left for the night, and as I sat by Michael's bed, holding his hand while his chest rose and fell with slower and slower breaths, my conviction faltered.

My brother's slitted eyes either meant he was near death or he was still with me. I shook his hand. "Michael?"

His slitted eyes opened. "I here, Yo-anna."

"I'll be right back, okay?"

"O—" One slow breath. Two slow breaths. "O-kay."

I ran from the house, releasing the tears I'd been holding back. On Jared's porch, I banged on the screen door. "Fanny? Is Jared here?"

After opening the door, Fanny raised a hand to her mouth. "Oh, no. Has Michael …?"

"It won't be long. I'd like Jared to be with us."

"He's in his room. Isaac's in town." Fanny hurried down the hall, her blue dress swirling about her legs, and knocked on a door. "Jared, it's Michael. Joanna needs you."

The door opened. Jared burst out, a boot in each hand. In the kitchen, he sat at the table to put them on. "I didn't think it would be this soon, Joanna."

I took a napkin from the holder on the table and wiped my eyes, while Jared tied his bootlaces. When he was done, it took less than a minute before we were sitting at Michael's bedside. He opened his eyes. "Hey, Ja-red. Not long ... not long now."

Jared's Adam's apple bobbed up and down. "You're a faithful man, Michael. I admire you more than I can say."

"Need ... need you ... need you to promise."

"Anything, anything at all."

"Take care of ..." One slow breath, then another. "Take care Yo-anna. She love you. I see. You love ... you love her, too."

Jared nodded. "I pro—" His voice broke. "I promise."

The slightest of smiles raised Michael's lips. "Yo-anna ... hand." I held Michael's left hand, which rested on his chest. "Ja-red ... hand." Jared held Michael's right hand, also on his chest. Mustering the last of his strength, Michael joined our hands together. "There. Now ... now say it."

Over the slowing chest of my sweet brother, my brown eyes and Jared's blue eyes met. As if we were of one mind, we whispered, "I love you."

Michael's hands fell to his chest. Although his slitted eyes closed, his chest continued to rise and fall. I squeezed Jared's hand. "I'm sorry. I didn't know he was going to do that."

Jared eased his hand away. "It's all right. I told you at Christmas I'd do anything for you and Michael, like I'd do anything for anyone in my community."

I settled back into my chair, exhausted from finally admitting my love for an Amish man I could never marry. Leave it to my brother to force me to do that on his deathbed. Like Jared, though, I didn't mind.

If there was one thing I wanted more than marrying him, it was to give Michael peace during our final moments together.

Two days later, as I sat alone in the front row of chairs beneath a blue funeral home tent, my minister finished the service. Between work and Michael, I had no close friends. Some of our parents' friends attended, and I was grateful. Jared, Isaac, Fanny, Bishop Bontrager, and my boss also attended, and I was grateful for them, too.

The minister shook my hand, offering his condolences and saying to please return to church when I could. My boss rounded the empty chairs behind me and said to take as much time from work as I needed. My parents' friends offered their condolences, paused at their graves, and followed my boss to the parking lot.

April sunlight glinted off the headstones. The smell of fresh-cut grass filled the air. On Michael's coffin, which rested on the platform above the grave, a breeze caressed the wildflower spray I'd bought. To one side of the cemetery, beneath the limbs of a huge oak, two men waited beside a backhoe to fill the grave.

My faith raised my hand to Michael's coffin. In the shade of the tent, the sky-blue metal felt cool. I'd wanted a wood coffin, but the graveside service was expensive enough without it, not to mention the lack of a funeral home visitation. An Amish funeral, as Bishop Bontrager had suggested, would've cost less. I never mentioned it to Michael because I thought he'd rather be with our parents. Who knew where'd I'd end up? Not in an Amish cemetery, I was sure.

When my three-day bereavement leave ended, I returned to work to pay my bills. The car rental, which I'd extended, and propane bills were bad enough. Now I had a funeral service to pay for. At least my house rental was reasonable. If not, I wouldn't have been able to find peace on the porch, watching Jared and Isaac plow fields and plant crops.

At the end of each day, after I ate a microwave dinner, I debated on whether to finish unpacking the cardboard boxes in the back room. Jared hadn't mentioned Susan lately. If they weren't going to court or marry, they wouldn't need to live here, if that was their plan.

I clung to that belief until September, when Jared came to the porch one night.

Corn harvesting season had started. The men of the community took turns helping each household, and they had done so that day at this farm, cutting and bundling the stalks to grind for silage for livestock feed.

I admired how they helped each other, and I sometimes yearned for such a simple life. For breaks, Fanny offered lemonade on the porch. For lunch, the wives of the men served dishes I could smell without seeing, likely chicken casserole and apple pie.

More corn stalks fell. More were

bundled and stacked on wagons. The sun dropped toward the horizon. The field emptied, both of men and corn, leaving only stubble to be covered by winter storms until it was plowed under in the spring.

At the refrigerator, I pondered my choices, eventually choosing a microwave dinner like I'd mentioned earlier. No sooner than I'd finished the last bite did I hear the unmistakable sound of boots clomping up my steps and across the porch, followed by someone's knuckles tapping the screen door. "Joanna, it's Jared. Can I come in?"

I threw the dinner container away and opened the door.

Earlier, on the way to his house after harvesting corn, Jared had plodded along, worn out and sweating through his black pants and light blue shirt. He now wore fresh clothes and had bathed, evidenced by his damp curls and the aroma of soap on his skin. "If I'm bothering you, we can talk later."

I didn't care for his firm tone. "Now's fine. I just finished eating."

I sat at the kitchen table. He sat across from me. "We haven't talked about this, but do you have any idea how long you'll stay here?"

I clenched my teeth hard enough to bite a corn stalk in two. "We didn't sign a lease, remember?" I shook my head. "I can't believe this. You're actually going to marry someone you don't love." I looked away and back. "I haven't seen Susan here. She didn't even help with lunch like the other ladies did. Are you going to marry her without courting her?"

Jared's lips slowly parted. "I don't mean to upset you. She and I have been talking. She seems to have changed. She's kind and generous and hasn't mentioned anything physical before marriage. She still wants to marry on Christmas, so …"

"So you'll marry someone you don't love," I blurted. "I told you before, that's not fair to Susan. Have you talked to Bishop Bontrager about it? I'm sure he'll agree with me."

Silence fell over the table, until Jared's cheek twitched. "He, umm … I'd rather not say. We Amish don't discuss personal things like this."

"Really? As close as we've been, and as many things as we've talked about, you say that now? I guess you're a liar like Susan lied, when she used Jacob to make you jealous."

Jared clasped his hands together. "What have I lied about?"

"You told Michael your Christmas was special because we came into your life. That was a lie, wasn't it? The first chance you get, you want to kick me out of my own home."

"Joanna, I—"

I don't want to hear it," I said, aiming my finger at the door. "Leave. As soon as I can find somewhere to go, I'll pack and get out of your life for good."

Head down, eyes blinking, Jared walked out the door. I listened to his boots clomp across the porch and down the steps, hopefully for the last time.

Yes, that was anger talking. Not only did I love him, I'd likely never love another man again. When you give your whole heart to a person, no pieces are left for anyone else.

September became October. October become November. Instead of giving Jared the rent check, I sent it in the mail. Isaac and Fanny asked what was going on between us. This surprised me because Jared should've told them about marrying Susan. I told them nothing was going on that I knew of, and they seemed to accept that answer. If they'd asked him the same question, I didn't know his answer. Like he'd said, the Amish didn't discuss personal issues, so maybe he wasn't ready to discuss his pending wedding.

As far as a new home, I'd found a small apartment a few miles from the clinic. As far as Amish weddings, I'd overheard a few ladies talking about some recent ones while shopping in the grocery. I guess no one told them about not discussing personal issues.

Me and my anger. Then again, I knew my broken heart was making me think unkind things. The sooner I moved, the better. Then Jared and I could get on with our lives—his of a loveless marriage, mine of a loveless life.

A week before Thanksgiving, as I was packing for the move, I opened the cardboard boxes Jared had helped me bring in. When I raised the flaps, I thought someone was playing a joke on me. Then, without the least bit of warning, I remembered something Isaac had mentioned about a little Amish girl Jared liked as a child. Confusion twined through me like a spider's web twines through wildflowers on a spring afternoon

I closed the box and rubbed my forehead. Could it be a joke? Not likely.

Could my memory of what Isaac said be mistaken? It was possible. Regardless of my questions, only one person could answer them, and I'd go see that person right this minute.

Chapter 11

Jared

The day I asked Joanna if she could move, Isaac asked what was wrong during supper. Before I could answer, Fanny asked the same thing. "And what was all that yelling about?" she added, sitting beside Isaac after bringing a pan of rolls from the oven.

I dreaded their questions, but they deserved an answer. "I asked if she had plans to move."

"I'd reconsider proposing to Susan again," Isaac said. "Didn't you learn anything from how she lied to you about

Jacob?"

I spooned butterbeans. My frustration made me shove several off the plate. "I told you both I thought she'd changed."

Thankfully, the conversation ended then and there. Isaac knew how I felt about the matter, so I considered it closed. Come Thanksgiving, I'd propose to Susan again, and we'd tell her folks that night.

From September to November, nervousness about my decision clung to me like cockleburs clinging to my pants while I walked through a field. Then, the week before Thanksgiving, Bishop Bontrager came calling, saying he need to speak with me on an urgent matter. Wondering if Susan had told him we were considering courting again, I asked him in, adding if he'd like something to drink.

"*Denke*, no," he said, removing his straw hat and dropping it to the kitchen table. "Sit. As I said, this is urgent."

I sat. "I assume this is about Susan."

Above the bishop's dark beard, his eyes softened. "I realize my coming here to speak about such things isn't normal. I wouldn't do it if I didn't care about you like I care for everyone in our community." He fingered the brim of the hat. "I must ask you a question, and you must be honest. Do you love Susan? If you do, I'll never ask you again, but I have reason to believe you don't."

Joanna wouldn't tell him something so personal, so I had no idea what he meant.

"I see the answer in your eyes, Jared. I also saw it when you and Joanna and I spoke about her renting your *dawdi haus*. You don't love Susan because you love Joanna, *jah?*"

What an unexpected question to be asked. "That's … it's … how can you ask me such a thing when she's not Amish?"

Bishop Bontrager patted my hand on the table. "I've often preached about faith. Do you have faith, Jared?"

"How can I have faith when it's impossible for Joanna and I to marry?" I asked, hearing my own rising voice. "I want to marry. I want a family. Susan and I will find love eventually. That's what I have faith in."

"Hmm, that's not the answer I hoped to hear. No matter what, no matter how impossible something seems, you're supposed to have faith in *Gott*." He faced the screen door. "Isn't that right, Joanna?"

The door opened, revealing a young woman wearing a white kapp, a blue dress, a white apron, and white tennis shoes. She came in and sat beside Bishop Bontrager. "You're exactly right, Bishop. Without our faith in God, how can we have faith in anyone else?"

Despite my shaking legs, I stood. "What kind of joke is this? How dare you wear those clothes." I faced the bishop. "What has she told you? Did she put you up to this?"

"Honesty put us up to this, Jared. Calm

down and sit. Faith has come full circle in Joanna's life. Now it will come full circle in yours, if you let it."

I dropped into the chair. Regardless of Bishop Bontrager's sincere words, doubts filled my head, especially the doubt of Joanna wearing Amish clothes. No one could become Amish in the blink of an eye. It takes commitment. It takes honesty. It takes love for your community. What kind of game was she playing? More importantly, how could Bishop Bontrager take part in it?

Joanna laughed. "He sure is thinking hard. Look at those squinting eyes."

"Well," the bishop said, "I suppose it's time to get serious. Jared, back to my question. Do you love Susan, or do you love someone else?"

I glared at Joanna. "What did you tell him?"

"Something you're not good at," she said, this time without humor. "The truth, unless you're ready to admit you love me."

Closing my eyes, I rubbed my forehead. "If there's one person in this world who can *ferhoodle* my brain, it's you."

"*Ach!*" the bishop said, grinning. "That means he loves you."

I opened my eyes and lowered my hand. "Yes! I admit it! I love her! Are you happy now?"

Bishop Bontrager faced Joanna. "It's about time."

"I agree," she said. "He sure is hardheaded. I don't know if I want to marry him or not." Joanna removed the kapp and lowered it to the table between us. "Remember the boxes you helped me bring in? The ones the new owners of my house brought?"

"The ones in the room with the Christmas ornaments?"

"That's right. I opened one of the boxes this morning and found a woman's Amish clothes. One more held the same thing. The other two held a man's Amish clothes."

"And?"

Joanna ran her fingers through her hair, which now curled a bit at the ends. "Isaac said you once liked a little Amish girl. Did she have curly hair?"

At the memory of the little girl, the tension in my face eased. "Much curlier than yours. I think she's one of my first memories. I couldn't have been more than three or four. She was too young to wear a kapp."

"Do you remember her name?" Bishop Bontrager asked?

I shook my head. "Why all the questions about something that happened so long ago?"

The bishop nodded at Joanna. "We'd better clear this up for him." He faced me. "Joanna came to see me after she opened the boxes. When she started asking me about her parents, I remembered a couple named Weaver. Like myself, your folks, and several others in the community, they were frustrated with the current bishop because he wasn't teaching us how faith in Jesus is what we need to enter Heaven. Her folks said they were going to become *Englisch* and left our community in Ohio. Until I spoke with Joanna today, I didn't know they moved to Lancaster. That little girl was Joanna."

"They must've taken being English almost as seriously as they took following Jesus," Joanna said. "It's kind of hazy, but after I saw those clothes, I think I remember them speaking with a Dutch accent. The more I thought about it, I think I also remember them practicing to speak without it. By the time I was old enough to ask them about it, I'd forgotten it."

Joanna reached across the table to take my hand. "Like the people in your community, I love Jesus with all my heart. He strengthened me when my parents died. He strengthened Michael to deal with his diagnosis and death. He strengthened me when my sweet brother died." Joanna studied me. "Because of God, my cup overflows with faith. We met as children all those years ago, and we found each other again." A single tear ran down her cheek, until it trembled on her quivering chin. "Where's your faith, Jared? I have enough faith in our love to become Amish. Don't you have enough faith to believe me?"

For several beats of my pounding heart, I was stunned into silence. If what she and Bishop Bontrager were saying was true, my life, as well as Joanna's life, was about to drastically change. "Are you really willing to become Amish?" I asked. Before she could answer, I faced Bishop Bontrager. "What about her job? Can she still be a nurse?"

"I've given that some thought," he said, stroking his beard. "The women in our community have many kinds of jobs, both here and in town."

"Except," Joanna said, tapping the kapp with a fingertip, "they wear Amish dresses and kapps. In my clinic, the nurses wear a specific uniform. Most everyone in Lancaster knows the Amish stop attending school in the eighth grade. If I wear Amish clothes, my patients might question my education, and I wouldn't blame them. They have to trust me, and they can trust me better if I wear the same clothes I've worn since I became a nurse."

Bishop Bontrager chuckled. "I understand. Imagine how my community would feel if I shaved my beard and wore blue jeans and a ball cap."

Although I laughed along with him and Joanna, I soon stopped because of another subject. "*Ach,*" I mumbled. "This will break Susan's heart."

"Let me speak with her," Bishop Bontrager said. "I thought you would propose last year, but I knew something was wrong between you two when you stopped taking her on buggy rides after volleyball games."

"What will you tell her?" Joanna asked.

"It isn't right to let someone else say my words for me," I said. "We talked about courting again, but I never asked her. In fact, in all our time together, I never told her I loved her."

"And if she's like most women," Joanna said, "she wouldn't want to marry a man who doesn't love her."

Satisfied with my plan, I faced Bishop Bontrager. "Do you think Joanna can take her vows soon?"

He raised one eyebrow at Joanna. "Unless I miss my guess, a certain young man wants to have a Christmas wedding." He reached over to pat my shoulder. "I would like to say it's possible, but next Christmas is more likely. As you know, studying to take vows to our *Ordnung* isn't something that happens overnight. Also, a year will give everyone time to get to know

Joanna."

"And it will give us plenty of time to plan our wedding," Joanna said. A cute grin quirked the corners of her mouth upward. "Now, what I want to know is are you going to keep charging your fiancé rent on the *dawdi haus*?"

Of course, my answer was I would not. As all three of us laughed, I silently thanked *Gott* for His many blessings. Yes, indeed, mine and Joanna's faith, as Bishop Bontrager had said, had come full circle.

The following year was filled with blessing after blessing. The most important blessing was how Susan understood we shouldn't marry since I didn't love her. She did shed some tears. Then I said she would find someone who would love her like she would love him, because she'd learned through our talks that physical affection isn't what true love is. That ended her tears, and she added how she might not have learned that if we hadn't courted.

The next blessing was our community accepting Joanna as a candidate to take her vows. They were a little puzzled when she came to her first Amish church service. After the sermon and before the meal following it, Bishop Bontrager asked her to join him at the front of the room. With her at his side, wearing a dress she once wore to her old church, he explained who she and Michael were, including how her folks used to live in our old community long ago.

Several people recalled her folks. What surprised them even more was when they found out we planned to marry after she took her vows.

The best part of the day came after the meal, when Susan apologized to Joanna for all the trouble that day at the *dawdi haus*. The second best part was when she said Jacob Graber wanted to court her.

The next blessing came a few weeks before Thanksgiving. Fanny and Isaac would be parents soon, and all four of us were having coffee and dessert after supper, at the large table in the huge house our folks had built. Joanna and Fanny already considered themselves to be best friends, so it came as no surprise when Fanny asked her if she wanted to feel the baby kick. Sitting beside her, Joanna pressed her hand to Fanny's stomach. After a few seconds, she smiled as her hand rose. "That's an active little boy or girl you have there, Fanny."

"I know. Our midwife passed away last year. Isaac has been wanting me to see a doctor. I suppose I should."

"I can recommend someone if you'd like," Joanna said.

"What about you?" Isaac asked. He snapped his fingers. "I know. Instead of you and Jared living in the *dawdi haus,* you can live here and make it a clinic. Everyone in our community would love having a nurse close by."

"That's a fine idea," I said. "It'd be much

more convenient than having to go into town to be treated for minor accidents and illnesses."

Fanny stopped listening to me and faced Joanna. "Can you deliver babies? I helped the midwife a few times. The worst part was the screaming. I thought about becoming one, but the blood made my stomach flip."

"*Daed* said *Mamm's* screams frightened him terribly," I said. I grinned at Isaac. "You'll have to give Fanny a piece of leather to put between her teeth."

Fanny shook her head at me. "You men would scream worse than a woman, and you know it."

We all enjoyed the humor in Fanny's words. Regardless, another blessing was the eventual opening of our community's first medical clinic, run by Joanna with Fanny assisting when she wasn't busy with children or house work. The pay at the Lancaster clinic was too good to let go, so Joanna planned to work there part time.

Let me get back to Joanna's vows. She took them in October and was welcomed into our community with a delicious meal afterward. Most everyone knew of our plan to marry, but not when. As I strolled around, many asked if we'd set a date. Despite the Amish custom of not discussing engagements, I felt blessed to do so, and gladly mentioned our plan to marry on Christmas day. Before I knew it, our community decided to combine our Christmas meal with our wedding. Joanna, to say the least, had felt a bit concerned about being welcomed into her new family, but the news made her feel right at home.

Approaching me with a whoopie pie, she smiled. "Who would've imagined I'd become Amish and marry an Amish man?"

I returned the smile. "Michael imagined it, remember?"

Joanna touched the white kapp. "I'm still having a hard time getting used to the clothes. I'm glad Bishop Bontrager's going to let me wear my nurse's uniform with my kapp when I open the clinic. A dress past my knees will get in the way."

I took her by the elbow and led her to a quiet corner. "We should visit Michael and thank him for his faith in us. I just wish he could be here for the wedding."

Joanna looked around. As I was about to ask why, she stood on tiptoe and kissed my cheek. "I know what you mean, but I'm sure he approves."

I waited while she nibbled the whoopie pie. "Will the clinic keep us from starting a family soon? It'd be *wunderbaar* if our children could grow up with Isaac's and Fanny's children."

"It would be." Joanna licked the cream filling from her lips. "But as we know, God will decide when we have children, not us."

Unconcerned with who might see us, I kissed her cheek. "Exactly the answer I'd expect from my faithful wife-to-be."

Between October and Christmas, with

Joanna acting as midwife, Isaac and Fanny welcomed twin babies into the world, a son named Eli and a girl named Rebecca. To say all four of us were happy would be a huge understatement, but our blessings grew beyond measure on our wedding day.

With our community's decision to follow the teachings of Jesus, we had built a large community center not far from Bishop Bontrager's farm. We gathered there for singings, meals, and worship, and now we gathered there for its first wedding.

Susan had become great friends with Joanna and Fanny, even becoming interested in working at the clinic when it opened. While my *bruder* and I, wearing our best Sunday clothes, waited for the ladies to put the final touches on Joanna's outfit in an adjacent room, Jacob joined us. "Are you nervous, Jared?"

Isaac elbowed him. "Does that mean you've proposed to Susan? It's about time, after all those months of courting."

Jacob nervously tugged his suspenders. "I suppose it does."

"'Suppose?'" I asked. "Aren't you sure?"

"Oh, I am, I am. You'll admit, though, going from single to married will be a big change."

"A change you'll cherish," Isaac said. He waved a hand at Eli and Rebecca, asleep in their double stroller beside him. "There's nothing like becoming a *daed*."

Bishop Bontrager came over. "Jared, if you'll join me at the front or the room, I've been told Joanna is ready."

It had been a long day—up early for chores, followed by a quick breakfast, bathing and dressing to arrive here at eight o'clock, listening to the bishop's two-hour sermon, his private counseling with Joanna and I about marriage and the congregation's singing—and I was ready to say our vows, eat, help clean up, and to receive our wedding gifts. Still, I was curious about whatever Joanna was doing in the adjacent room. She was already wearing her *mamm's* blue dress, black cape, white apron, and kapp. What else did she need for our ceremony?

Attempting to swallow the unexpected nervousness filling my throat, I followed the bishop. At his side, near the crackling embers in a huge fireplace, I turned to face the door of the adjacent room.

Jared, dressed in black pants, a white shirt, and a black coat like mine, joined me. "Why are you so pale, *bruder?*"

I smirked at him. "You should know. You were pale before you married Fanny."

The door opened, and the sight of Joanna took my breath away. Although she still wore her *mamm's* clothes, either Fanny or Susan had woven two bracelets of blue, yellow, and purple wildflowers around her wrists. She also held a bouquet of the same flowers in both hands. Since Amish ladies can't wear jewelry, I thought the bracelets made of flowers were a nice touch, but the most beautiful thing about Joanna was her lovely smile as she slowly walked toward me to take her place at my side.

Fanny and Susan stood a few steps away, to Joanna's left. "The flowers were my idea," Fanny whispered. She faced Bishop Bontrager. "I think us ladies deserve to wear a little nature now and then, don't you?"

"I see nothing wrong with it at all, Fanny. After all, we honor all of *Gott's* creation, even if it came from the florist because it's winter."

I expected him to open the Bible he held at his side. Instead, he faced everyone in our community—*daeds* and *mamms*, some with children, some with babies, some with both, some without, many youths in their teens, along with many elderly couples scattered about the room.

"Before I start, I'd like to say how blessed we are as a community. After we came here to worship in our own way, by following Jesus and His teachings, our small number has increased. I'm pleased with how we've changed our *Ordnung* to meet our needs, never straying from our faith. You've shown this by accepting Joanna as one of our own, come full circle to be with us again, not only as Jared's wife but as midwife and nurse of our community. *Denke* to you all for your kindness. It does my heart *wunderbaar gute* to be part of our community."

His focus returned to Joanna and me. "Faith in *Gott* and His Son is an amazing thing. It gave Michael the strength to face his illness with dignity and character. It gave him the insight to recognize the love between both of you when you placed the angel on your Christmas tree."

His focus went past us. "Everyone here knows we Amish are plain people, but in honor of Michael and of the symbol of Jesus's birth, the angel of the Lord, if anyone would care to decorate a large tree for Christmas, my ministers and I have no objection. All we ask is to do so like Joanna has done with her bracelets, with nature in mind."

Murmurs filled the room, most followed by smiles and nodding heads. "We can have a Christmas tree?" several children asked their parents.

Bishop Bontrager raised his hands. "Please settle down. We can discuss that another time."

He faced Joanna and me. "Yours is an interesting union. Joanna, last year at this time, you were *Englisch,* but we've welcomed you into our community. This is a rare occurrence, which gives me faith that *Gott* has blessed it."

He shared a soft smile. "We've not spoken of this. Although our wedding vows are simple, they are similar to the vows of the *Englisch.*" He smiled again, this time with a hint of humor. "Until now, no Amish couple here has kissed after their vows. Since you've been *Englisch* for most of your life, I'll leave that up to you and Jared. As I've said, our community came here to welcome new ideas. I've spoken with my ministers about it, and we see a chaste kiss as a fine way to confirm the vows you are about to make to each other."

He opened his Bible. "Can you both confess that God has ordained marriage to be a union between one man and one wife, and do you also have the confidence that you are approaching marriage in accordance with the way you have been taught?"

"Yes," I said.

"Yes," Joanna said.

"Jared, do you also have the confidence, *Bruder*, that the Lord has provided this, our *Schwester*, as a marriage partner for you?"

"Yes," I said.

"Joanna, do you also have the confidence, *Schwester*, that the Lord has provided this, our *Bruder*, as a marriage partner for you?"

"Yes," Joanna said.

"Jared, do you also promise your wife that if she should become in bodily weakness, sickness, or in any similar circumstances need your help, that you will care for her as is fitting for a Christian husband?"

"Yes," I said, remembering how Joanna had cared for Michael so unwaveringly.

"Joanna, do you promise your husband the same thing, that if he should in bodily weakness, sickness, or any other similar circumstances need your help, that you will care for him as is fitting a Christian wife?"

"Yes," Joanna said, her voice quivering as she likely remembered caring for her dear *bruder*.

Bishop Bontrager turned a page. "Do you promise together that you will come with love, forbearance and patience live with each other, and not part from each other until God will separate you in death?"

"Yes," Joanna and I said together."

Bishop Bontrager closed his Bible. "Congratulations. You are now husband and wife."

Taking Joanna's hands, I faced her.

"Go ahead," Isaac said, chuckling. "You know you want to."

Joanna stepped closer. "Why not? I think everyone here expects it."

I leaned down, gave her a quick kiss, and straightened. "I love you , Joanna. You make me so happy."

She reached up to press her palm to my cheek, then brushed a tear from it with her thumb. "Now those are the kinds of tears I like, happy tears."

"Oh, my," Fanny said, fingering her eyes. "You two make me wish I could get married all over again."

Bishop Bontrager offered a final prayer and blessed the food. Some guests started lining up at the tables, while some gathered around us, saying how wonderful the ceremony was.

Later, after the meal, we were given wedding gifts. Clumsy men that Isaac and I were, we had chipped many of our dishes, so a new set was welcome. A handmade quilt would keep Joanna and me warm on long winter nights, and a huge casserole dish would hold enough food to feed all four of us.

When the line dwindled, Joanna helped the ladies clean up. While Isaac and I swept the huge room, Bishop Bontrager donned his heavy coat and came over to clap me on the shoulder. "I'm very happy for you and Joanna, Jared. She's a *wunderbaar* young woman. I look forward to the opening of our new clinic." He started toward the door and stopped. "I also look forward to everyone gathering to build your new home in the clearing you told me about. It'll be a fine place to live." He winked. "Especially when the pond you plan to have has fish to catch."

Isaac stopped sweeping. "And I look forward to knowing Fanny will be in good hands when we have more children."

We said our goodbyes, continued to sweep the floor, and joined our wives when we were through. Soon, all six of us, myself and Joanna in front, Isaac and Fanny in back with Eli and Rebecca, were on our way home in the buggy. The air was crisp as random flakes of snow fell through the beams of light shining from the LED fixtures on the front of the enclosed buggy.

The following spring, when the snow blanketing the countryside began melting, Joanna and I finally did something we'd been wanting to do, which was to visit the cemetery where her folks and Michael were buried.

Beside me in the enclosed buggy, wearing her Amish clothes and a black cape over her shoulders, Joanna held a box wrapped with Christmas paper and tied with a bow. I hadn't mentioned how we were supposed to wrap presents with plain paper, evidenced by our wedding presents. This was a special occasion, so I understood completely.

We'd left right after breakfast. In the frigid morning, with sunlight illuminating frost on the leafless trees, we passed patches of snow on the roadsides. When we entered a close patch of woods, the clip-clop, clip-clop of Nick's rapid trot echoed back to us. In these shaded spots, with sunlight piercing the bare limbs, the colder air burned my sinuses, reminding of the smell of steel.

Thirty minutes later, a few miles southeast of Lancaster, we arrived at the cemetery. I parked the buggy by the church and held the wrapped box while Joanna climbed down. Safely on the pavement, she took the box, and we walked in the frostbitten grass, brown and crunching, between the gleaming headstones to

Michael's grave.

Joanna ran her fingertips over the polished granite, the same as her folks' headstones. Taking a cue from our Amish customs, she'd kept the inscription somewhat on the simple side, leaving off his actual birth and death dates.

Michael A. Weaver

Son and Brother

Friend and Inspiration

1999-2024

Joanna let me hold the box while she unwrapped it. Done with that part, she took out the very same angel she and I had put on the Christmas tree so many months ago. "Put the box down." Not knowing what to expect, I did. She placed the ribbon and paper inside it and stood to offer me the angel. "Remember how Michael wanted us to put it on the tree at the same time?"

She was holding the wing of the angel with her left hand. I gently held its right wing. "Like this, right?"

After she nodded, we placed the angel on the top of Michael's headstone. "I would ask if he knows what we're doing," she said quietly, "but I know he does."

"And your folks, too," I said.

Hand in hand we stood there, both silent, both, I was sure, considering the path of faith that had brought us together.

A few long moments passed. A breeze fluttered the ties of Joanna's kapp. She tipped her head back. "Jared! Look!"

I followed her gaze into the blue sky, surprised yet comforted at what we saw. Above us, a single cloud resembled an angel, her wings and dress spread in billowing white.

Smiling at Joanna, I slipped my arm around her shoulders and pulled her close. "*Jah*, love. Michael knows *exactly* what we're doing."

Dear reader,

Thank you for choosing this book. If you enjoyed reading it as much as I enjoyed writing it, you *really* enjoyed it. Saying that, please enjoy the first chapter of my first Amish Christmas book, The Forgiveness Quilt: An Amish Christmas Story.

Thank you for reading.

Chapter 1

Like a glowing ember pulsing with heat, the dull pain in Ruth Raber's lower back flared and dimmed, flared and dimmed. She rolled over in bed to face the window, where the *tic-tic* of sleet and a gray dawn announced a new day. Taking her equally gray braid in her fingers, she started to loosen it but stopped. After cleaning the house so thoroughly yesterday, she deserved a few more minutes beneath the warm covers. Besides, the brightening light outside meant the sleet was mixed with snow, which must have blanketed the yard overnight. This meant she had no intention of harnessing Lucy to the buggy and going anywhere for anything.

Her left hand, seemingly on its own, slid to the other pillow to find the head of the husband she had never married. For the time it took to blink an eye, despair entered her heart, until gratitude for *Gott's* love forced it away. Just opening one's eyes every day was a blessing. One could hurt, cry, hunger for love and companionship here on earth, or one could find the positive in all things. Ruth knew this was difficult for her to do, but she didn't quite know why.

Breath rasped in her throat. Her chest

rose and fell, rose and fell. Birthdays and more birthdays. How old was she now?

At sixteen, at her first gathering, when the youth of her community attended singings to find a potential husband or wife to court, she had sat across from the table from Thomas Yoder. He wasn't particularly handsome, but her parents said he was a hard worker who had already decided to forgo *Rumschpringe* and be baptized into the church as soon as he turned eighteen. This was acceptable to Ruth, therefore her decision to sit across from him.

Then, without a word, he had moved to another table.

Ruth did the same thing for every singing until her eighteenth birthday, choosing a different boy each time with the same results each time. That summer, as she walked home behind *Daed*, *Mamm*, and Timothy, her *bruder*, she prayed and prayed to understand the boys' lack of interest in her. She read the Bible often. She went to church with her family each and every time. She had learned to cook and clean and sew and make baskets and garden as well as any other girl in her community, but none of that made any difference.

Wind howled around the corners of the house. Branches from the oak outside her bedroom clattered against the wall. In their stalls in the barn, Lucy whinnied and the milk cow mooed. Their water was frozen and they had eaten their hay and feed. The weather was even keeping the rooster in the henhouse. Big Red himself didn't care for winter any more than Ruth did, evidenced by his lack of crowing.

In the window, the light grew brighter. The snow must be several inches thick by now. The *tic-tic* of the sleet stopped. A beam of sunlight burst through the glass, illuminating the curtain: thin, white, and plain. Then the sky faded back to gray. Huge snowflakes, like drifting leaves coated with frost, followed, visible even through the thin curtain. Other than *Gott*, who knew how deep the snow would get before it ended.

The horse whinnied and the cow mooed again. Better get up and tend to them before the snow deepened.

As Ruth rolled over to sit on the side of the bed, the pain in her back stabbed deep into the muscle, making her gasp. Her breath rasped again. Her heart galloped wildly in her chest. *I'm ready when you call, Lord. Other than existing on this earth, I've had little reason to come into this world.*

Another pain, this one in her chest, said a heart attack might happen at any time. The thudding boom in her ears said a stroke might occur as well. The dark growth on her nose said skin cancer might take her also. Only the Lord knew which one it would be.

Wearing the black leather shoes and black dress and bonnet of her Old Order

Amish community, she donned a heavy coat and opened the back door. A gust of icy wind swirled snow beneath the porch. Despite the edges of the bonnet extending past her face as if she were peering from within a dark tunnel, flakes stuck in her eyebrows, melted on her cheeks. She almost slipped and fell on the steps but kept her balance. The snow came to her ankles, an icy crust of sleet crunching on top. One step, two steps, five. She shook her head. Her gloves, she had forgotten her gloves. Her arthritic fingers would be numb in minutes without them.

Ruth …

She looked up into the multitude of snowflakes, each as large as a hen's egg. She started to ask who had called her name, but a gust of wind stole the words from her freezing lips. The cancer must be growing in her brain; either that or old age was making her senile. Yes, indeed, what use did she have on this earth any longer? No beloved husband warmed her heart, her home, or her bed. No beloved children, grandchildren, or great-grandchildren visited on Thanksgiving or Christmas to say how much they loved her, to say how fine a cook she was, to say, "What would we do without you, *Mammi?*"

Her shoes left trenches in the snow. Twice, she almost lost her footing in the crust of sleet. Behind her, the wind clattered the oak limbs as if they were the bones of *Daed* and *Mamm,* long dead now.

At the barn, when the deepening snow wouldn't let her open the door enough to allow any light inside, she shook her head again. She had forgotten a kerosene lamp.

Ruth ...

Through the narrow gap between the barn door and the wall, she peeked into the darkness inside. No one here. No one outside. Her grasp on reality must certainly be slipping.

The horse whinnied. The cow mooed. Regardless, she must have a lantern to find the pitchfork and—

Ruth shook her head again. The wooden cover over the well would be heavy with the snow and sleet, and the horse and cow needed water.

Ruth …

Breathing hard, each breath a cloud pluming from her mouth and nostrils, she squeezed through the narrow opening and stepped inside. Dust assailed her sense of smell, hay and manure too. To her left, somewhere in a corner, a mouse—or worse, a rat—scurried in the darkness. Despite the dim light penetrating the cracks in the overlapping boards here and there, each illuminating a haze of dust motes, Ruth couldn't see the pitchfork. Running her hands along the walls, she felt everything but: a shovel and a hoe for gardening, a rake for gathering oak leaves in the fall, a scythe for cutting corn stalks after the golden ears were picked.

She stopped to lean her aching back against the horse's stall door. Lucy whinnied and snorted; the cow mooed.

Ruth had no idea why she hadn't named the cow. Maybe she should now, before she died and the cow's new owner didn't know what to call her. A hoarse laugh erupted from Ruth's throat. What a silly thing to think. If she died out her in the barn, she wouldn't be able to tell anyone the cow's name.

She shivered. Her hands were freezing, fingers stiff. Even inside the barn, with what little light was available, she could see her breath cloud before her face. Inside the leather shoes, her toes were numb.

A gust of wind moaned. The barn's tin roof rattled. The oak limbs clattered. The door slammed shut, blown by the wind. Except for the light entering those cracks in the walls, darkness surrounded her. Fear clenched her throat. Terror gripped her heart. She gave a little cry—the cry of a child in the night afraid of the dark, hot tears streaming, soaking her pillow.

Whose memory was that? Certainly not hers. Or was it? Yes, but not the cry of a child. Rather, it was the cry of a young woman seeking—yet not finding—love. She remembered the afternoon Thomas Yoder moved to another table. At home that night, as she unpinned her hair, she studied her reflection in her bedroom window. Her eyes were honey-brown like the soil in her family's garden—a good thing. Her nose was upturned—cute as a button so *Daed* said—very nice so *Mamm* said. In private, years before, Timothy said she resembled a pig.

Several sings later, that night at home, *Daed* and *Mamm* whispered in their room about Ruth being too plain to attract a boy. At the window, she studied her face again. Timothy was right; she resembled a pig.

In bed, as tears streamed past her ears and wet her hair and pillow, she dreamed of a voice. *Ruth,* it called, *true beauty lies within the heart and soul through faith. Do not believe otherwise. A person who doesn't know this will make the years long and the heart lonely.* Those beautiful, booming words ended her tears. She climbed out of bed and knelt on the hard, wooden floor to thank *Gott* for his insight, and to ask forgiveness for her doubts.

In the stall, Lucy pawed the straw while the cow bumped the wall with her hip. Ruth shuffled to the barn door and shoved it open. She went back to get the shovel and slowly made her way to the well. After breaking the crust of sleet and scraping the snow from the wooden cover, she fetched the bucket from the barn, filled it and took it to the porch. Warm up inside first, then care for the animals. She stomped her feet, leaving little piles of snow gathered around her shoes. In the kitchen, she opened the door to the wood stove and almost cried. She had forgotten to add wood before bed last night, and the fire was nothing more than a few glowing embers the size of a fingernail. Even worse, she hadn't brought any wood inside or to the porch. Of course, it was stacked beneath a tarp behind the barn, another treacherous trip away.

Ruth, they're counting on you, you know. Don't let them down.

Ruth jerked her head up and glared at the ceiling. "If that's you, Lord, I'm sorry for my infirmity. I'm doing the best I can. Isn't that all anyone can do?"

No answer. No booming voice. Nothing but the near silent crackle of those few cooling embers sending a wisp of woodsmoke curling upward inside the stove.

Wary of her sore back, Ruth dragged a chair over from the kitchen table and eased into it. Snowmelt glistened on her shoes.

She held her hands over those barely pulsing embers. Once her hands were warm, she might be able to water and feed the animals, gather wood and make breakfast, including a pot of steaming coffee. With plenty of sugar and cream, it was her one weakness.

She frowned sourly, feeling the wrinkles in her face fold. No, her other weakness was always believing she resembled a pig, like Timothy had said.

Her hands gradually grew warm, the fingers becoming flexible. Sleep tugged her eyelids down. Sleep or death, whichever it was, she would welcome it.

Ruth, the booming voice said, *let's visit a Christmas past.*

J. Willis Sanders lives in southern Virginia, with his wife and several stringed musical instruments.

With over twenty books published and more on the way, he enjoys crafting intriguing characters and equally intriguing conflicts. He also loves the natural world, and, more often than not, his stories include those settings. Most also utilize intense love relationships and layered themes.

His first idea for novel, *The Coincidence of Hope,* is a ghostly World War II era historical that takes place mostly in the midwestern United States, which utilizes some little-known facts about German POW camps there at the time. It's the first of a three-book series, in which characters from the first continue their lives.

Although he loves history, he has written several contemporary novels as well, and some include interesting paranormal twists, both with and without religious themes.

He also loves the Outer Banks of North Carolina, and he has written several novels within different time frames based on the area, what he calls his Outer Banks of North Carolina Series. (Yes, he has more ideas for books about the area.)

As this book shows, he enjoys creating Amish characters. Some of these stores are traditional, like the Clara Engleman series and his Amish holiday series, while some, like the Eliza Gray series and the soon to start Vine series, step outside those traditional boundaries.

Other hobbies include reading (of course), vegetable gardening, playing music with friends, and songwriting, some of which are in a few of his novels.

To follow his work, visit any of these websites:

https://jwillissanders.wixsite.com/writer

https://www.facebook.com/J-Willis-Sanders-874367072622901

https://www.amazon.com/J-Willis-Sanders/e/B092RZG6MC?ref_=dbs_p_ebk_r00_abau_000000

Readers: to help those considering a purchase, please leave a review on Amazon.com, Goodreads.com, or wherever you bought this book.
They help authors more than you may realize.

Thank you.